SWITCH-HITTER

ALSO BY DEREK JETER

SWITCH-HITTER

DEREK JETER

with Paul Mantell

JETER CHILDREN'S

SIMON & SCHUSTER BOOKS FOR YOUNG READERS

New York   London   Toronto   Sydney   New Delhi

SIMON & SCHUSTER BOOKS FOR YOUNG READERS
An imprint of Simon & Schuster Children's Publishing Division
1230 Avenue of the Americas, New York, New York 10020
This book is a work of fiction. Any references to historical events, real people, or
real places are used fictitiously. Other names, characters, places, and events are
products of the author's imagination, and any resemblance to actual events or
places or persons, living or dead, is entirely coincidental.
Text © 2022 by Jeter Publishing, Inc.
Cover illustration © 2022 by Tim O'Brien
Cover design by Krista Vossen © 2022 by Simon & Schuster, Inc.
All rights reserved, including the right of reproduction in whole or in part in any form.
SIMON & SCHUSTER BOOKS FOR YOUNG READERS and related marks are
trademarks of Simon & Schuster, Inc.
For information about special discounts for bulk purchases, please contact Simon
& Schuster Special Sales at 1-866-506-1949 or business@simonandschuster.com.
The Simon & Schuster Speakers Bureau can bring authors to your live event. For
more information or to book an event, contact the Simon & Schuster Speakers
Bureau at 1-866-248-3049 or visit our website at www.simonspeakers.com.
Also available in a Simon & Schuster Books for Young Readers hardcover edition
Book design by Krista Vossen
The text for this book was set in Centennial LT.
Manufactured in the United States of America 0223 OFF
First Simon & Schuster Books for Young Readers paperback edition April 2023
2 4 6 8 10 9 7 5 3 1
The Library of Congress has cataloged the hardcover edition as follows:
Names: Jeter, Derek, 1974- author. | Mantell, Paul, author.
Title: Switch-hitter / Derek Jeter ; with Paul Mantell.
Description: First edition. | New York : Simon & Schuster Books for Young Readers,
[2022] | Series: [The contract series ; 9] | "Jeter Children's" | Audience: Ages 8-12
| Audience: Grades 4-6 | Summary: Seventh grader Derek Jeter, distracted with
responsibilities of playing both basketball and baseball, finds himself on the bench
with an injury and he must learn how to be a team player from the dugout and
understand the importance of taking care of his body.
Identifiers: LCCN 2021034256 (print) | LCCN 2021034257 (ebook)
ISBN 9781534499775 (hardcover) | ISBN 9781534499782 (pbk)
ISBN 9781534499799 (ebook)
Subjects: LCSH: Jeter, Derek, 1974—Childhood and youth—Juvenile fiction. |
CYAC: Jeter, Derek, 1974—Childhood and youth—Fiction. | Teamwork (Sports)—
Fiction. | Baseball—Fiction.
Classification: LCC PZ7.J55319 Sw 2022 (print) | LCC PZ7.J55319 (ebook) |
DDC [Fic]—dc23
LC record available at https://lccn.loc.gov/2021034256
LC ebook record available at https://lccn.loc.gov/2021034257

To Bella, Story, and River. I hope you find someone who inspires you and, when the time is right, I hope you are able to inspire others.

A Note About the Text

The rules of Little League followed in this book are the rules of the present day. There are six innings in each game. Every player on a Little League baseball team must play at least two innings of every game in the field and have at least one at bat. In any given contest, there is a limit on the number of pitches a pitcher can throw, in accordance with age. Pitchers who are eight years old are allowed a maximum of fifty pitches in a game, pitchers who are nine or ten years old are allowed seventy-five pitches per game, and pitchers who are eleven or twelve years old are allowed eighty-five pitches.

Dear Reader,

Switch-Hitter is inspired by some of my experiences growing up. The book portrays the values my parents instilled in me and the lessons they have taught me about how to remain true to myself and embrace the unique differences in everyone around me.

Switch-Hitter is based on the lesson that everything in life is an opportunity for both fun and learning. This is one of the principles I have lived by in order to achieve my dreams. I hope you enjoy reading!

Derek Jeter

DEREK JETER'S 10 LIFE LESSONS

1. Set Your Goals High (*The Contract*)

2. Think Before You Act (*Hit & Miss*)

3. Deal with Growing Pains (*Change Up*)

4. The World Isn't Always Fair (*Fair Ball*)

5. Find the Right Role Models (*Curveball*)

6. Don't Be Afraid to Fail (*Fast Break*)

7. Have a Strong Supporting Cast (*Strike Zone*)

8. Be Serious but Have Fun (*Wind Up*)

9. Be a Leader, Follow the Leader (*Switch-Hitter*)

10. Life Is a Daily Challenge

CONTRACT FOR DEREK JETER

1. Family Comes First. Attend our nightly dinner.
2. Be a Role Model for Sharlee. (She looks to you to model good behavior.)
3. Do Your Schoolwork and Maintain Good Grades (As or Bs).
4. Bedtime. Lights out at nine p.m. on school nights.
5. Do Your Chores. Take out the garbage, clean your room on weekends, and help with the dishes.
6. Respect Others. Be a good friend, classmate, and teammate. Listen to your teachers, coaches, and other adults.
7. Respect Yourself. Take good care of your body and your mind. Avoid alcohol and drugs. Surround yourself with positive friends with strong values.
8. Work Hard. You owe it to yourself and those around you to give your all. Do your best in everything that you do.
9. Think Before You Act.

Failure to comply will result in the loss of playing sports and hanging out with friends. Extra-special rewards include attending a Major League Baseball game, choosing a location for dinner, and selecting another event of your choice.

CONTENTS

Chapter One

A NEW SEASON

"Hey, old man. It's Vijay on the phone—for you!"

Derek Jeter dropped the pile of folded clothes he'd been holding. They fell right back into the suitcase he'd been unpacking, and he hurried downstairs to pick up the phone from his mom.

"Hey, Vij!" he said breathlessly. "How's it going?"

"It's all good now that *you're* back," said Vijay with a little laugh. "How was your trip home?"

"Long and boring," Derek said. "But the summer was good—always is."

"Hey, how about we meet up on the Hill, and you can tell me all about it?"

"Ah, I'd love to, but I'm just unpacking. Anyway, after twelve hours in the car, I'm kind of beat."

"Tomorrow after school, then?"

"For sure. Back to St. Augustine, huh? I can't believe school's already starting. I just got home."

"Well, that's what happens when you stay on vacation till the last minute," Vijay pointed out. "Anyway, see you in class."

"*Seventh grade.* Unreal, huh?"

"I know. Crazy. Where did all those years go?"

"Really. Well, see you tomorrow." Derek hung up, and turned to find his mom standing there, her arms crossed and an amused look on her face.

"Seventh grade," she said. "You two are all grown up!"

Derek laughed, but in a way it was true. He did feel suddenly grown-up, or at least on the verge of it.

In other places kids went to different schools starting in sixth or seventh grade. He was still at St. Augustine, so going back shouldn't have felt much different.

And yet somehow it did. Derek actually felt more nervous than usual about the first day of school. The workload in seventh grade was rumored to be a lot harder. And it was definitely going to be weird going back to school and not seeing *Dave* there.

Dave Hennum was Derek's other best friend besides Vijay. But in June the Hennum family had moved all the way to Hong Kong. Dave's dad had been transferred there for work, and the family was going to live there for the next two years.

Derek wondered how Dave was getting along, with all his friends so far away, and him living in a strange new place, where people mostly spoke a different language. (Although, Dave had assured him that they spoke English, too.)

Derek hadn't gotten a letter from him for over a month. In that time, Derek had sent Dave three letters—not easy, considering he didn't like letter writing to begin with.

During the summer he hadn't noticed Dave's absence much. Days at the lake in New Jersey with his dozens of cousins were full, noisy, and busy. He'd even gone into the city with his grandma a couple of times, to play ball with the city kids he'd met the summer before.

Overall he'd had his usual great time. He'd practically forgotten about Dave, except when Dave's letters had come—which hadn't happened since the end of July.

But now, back in Michigan and with school about to start again, things already felt different. Not having Dave around, it felt like a big part of Derek's world was gone, and it made him sad in a way he'd never felt before.

Just then, though, Derek's dad came into the house, carrying a white plastic tub full of mail. "The postman was here and dropped this off," he said, setting it down on the floor. "I saw your name on one or two envelopes."

Derek sat down beside the tub and started rifling through the piles of envelopes, magazines, and catalogs— four days' worth, from the time when his parents had taken off in the car to pick up Derek and his little sister,

Sharlee, and drive them home from New Jersey.

Soon Derek found the buried treasure he was looking for—two picture postcards from Dave, *and* a letter!

One postcard had a picture of a beautiful mountain, with skyscrapers crowding it from top to bottom. It was dated August 10—*four weeks ago*!

On the back of the card, Dave had written: "This is Victoria Peak, the most famous view in Hong Kong. We went up there on cable cars! It was cool, and a little scary. This place is amazing—very different from the States in a lot of ways, but the same in others."

That was it. There wasn't much room on the back of a postcard, after all.

The second card was dated August 15. It showed a beautiful golf course with a pagoda in front of it, and the same mountain, but in the distance this time. "This is the best golf course I've ever played," Dave had written on the back.

Golf was Dave's passion, in the same way that baseball was Derek's. That's why the two of them had always understood each other so well.

The rest of the postcard said: "My dad's company pays for his membership in the club, so I've already played there five times—in just three weeks! It's a hard course, but I love the challenge!"

Yup, thought Derek, smiling and shaking his head. *That's Dave, all right.*

But it was the *letter* that Derek wanted to see most.

Pictures were one thing, but he wanted to know what it was really like for Dave, being in another country thousands of miles away from America.

Derek couldn't imagine himself in that kind of situation. He hadn't moved since he was four years old—and he had no intention of moving again anytime soon!

The letter was dated August 25. It read:

Dear Derek,

Well, I finally have time to sit down and write to you. You wouldn't believe how busy it's been! I have Cantonese language classes after school—yes, school! They start here at the beginning of August! Can you believe it?

School is harder here than at St. Augustine, and the teachers are really strict too. My parents are always busy—my dad at work, my mom with starting up her own business—so they don't have much time to do stuff with me. And Chase isn't here, so I haven't had too much fun, other than golf.

Chase had been the Hennum family's driver and had often been in charge of watching Dave, since Mr. and Mrs.

Hennum were out working most of the time. But he hadn't joined the family in Hong Kong.

> The best times I've had here are on Sundays, when my parents and I go touring around the city and the harbor. There are floating markets, where it's crowded with boats, all loaded with stuff for sale. We brought home all kinds of foods we'd never seen before, let alone eaten! Most of them taste good, but some are not so great to look at—I'll leave it at that.

Derek had to laugh. Dave's sense of humor had obviously survived the trip to China.

> But the worst part is not being <u>back home</u>, with you and Vijay and the rest of the kids, hanging out on Jeter's Hill and playing ball, hitting golf balls at my house. . . . You know, all that stuff. I get sad sometimes, but I'm sure once I make some friends here, it will get easier.

Derek noticed that Dave still referred to Kalamazoo as "home." *Good.* That meant he still missed his old life, and his old *friends.* . . .

*Well, I guess that's all for now. You'll be
starting school soon, so at least I won't
have to be jealous anymore, ha-ha.*

Your friend,
Dave

Derek put the letter down on the table, next to the two postcards. He sat there thinking about what life was going to be like without Dave around. It made him feel at least a little better to know that Dave missed him, too.

But not *that* much better. Not as good as if Dave were still in Michigan.

"It's the bottom of the ninth, two on, two out, with the Tigers trailing by a pair, 3–1. The first-place Red Sox have won five straight, and they're looking for more. . . . Carsten takes a fastball for ball one. . . ."

"He's gonna drive 'em in," Derek's dad said confidently as Carsten let ball two go by. "You just watch, Derek."

Derek looked at his father sitting in his armchair, while Derek and Sharlee shared the couch, and Mom occupied the rocker in the corner. "How do you *know* that, Dad?"

"Don't believe me," Mr. Jeter said, a smile curling one corner of his mouth. "Just don't say I didn't warn you."

On the next pitch Carsten walloped a line drive into the right field corner. The runner on second scored, and the runner on first was rounding third. Derek and his dad were both yelling, "Go! Go!" Sharlee got up and danced on the couch, until Mrs. Jeter told her to quit it.

"How did you know, Daddy?" Sharlee asked. "How did you—"

But Mr. Jeter wasn't listening. He wasn't smiling, either. Kurt Carsten had pulled up lame before reaching second base. The throw came in to the second baseman, who tagged the limping Carsten out *before* the second runner crossed the plate.

Game over! Somehow the Tigers had snatched defeat from the jaws of victory!

"Well, that beats all," Mr. Jeter said disgustedly. "Why didn't he just stop at first if he was hurt?"

"Why would he do *that*, Dad?" Derek asked. "It was a double all the way."

"Because he's nursing a hamstring injury, that's why! You don't go full-out if you're protecting an injury. Not only did he cost us this game, but now he's going to miss a *bunch* of games—just watch—and for *what*?"

Derek was puzzled. He'd always played baseball full-out, running as hard and as fast as he could, diving for balls even if they were way out of reach. He couldn't conceive of a player holding back the way his father was suggesting!

They watched as Carsten limped off the field. "He already missed two weeks with it last month," said Mr. Jeter. "Now he's going to wind up missing half the stretch drive, and the team's going to have to catch Boston without him!" He shook his head. "He should have just sat on the bench and rested it every few games. But not Carsten. No, no—not him."

"He's their team leader, Dad! He's not going to sit down when the team needs him," Derek pointed out.

"And now the team's not going to have him for a longer period of time."

On the TV the on-field reporter caught up to Carsten just as he was about to hit the dugout. Mr. Jeter stood up.

"Where're you going, Dad?" Derek asked.

"I'm going to go grade some papers. This team drives me crazy."

"But, Dad—"

"Kurt," the reporter said, *"what happened out there?"*

Carsten shook his head sadly. *"I think I just pushed my body too hard."*

"Do you think the manager should have rested you longer?"

Carsten shrugged. *"I don't know,"* he said. *"We're in a pennant chase. I leaned on him to put me out there. So I guess that's on me."*

"You're the team leader," said the reporter. *"How are your teammates going to catch Boston now?"*

"I want to be out there every game, every inning," said Carsten. *"But we'll see what the doctors say. Even if I'm on the bench, I can still bring my energy to the dugout*

every day and cheer my guys on. If I can't set an example with my game, I can still notice things, and pass them along to my teammates—participate from the bench."

Mr. Jeter shook his head in dismay. Then he turned to Derek. "Did I ever tell you about when I hurt my knee in college?"

"Uh . . . a few times," Derek answered, looking from his mom to Sharlee. All of them had heard the story more than once and were trying not to laugh.

"Well, learn from other people's mistakes, Derek," said his dad, wagging his finger. "If you don't take care of your body, it won't take care of you."

Chapter Two

WORK AND PLAY

Derek saw Vijay the next morning on the school bus, but someone was already sitting next to him, and anyway, it was too noisy to catch up. Everyone was talking over everybody else, greeting friends they hadn't seen since June, telling new jokes they'd heard over the summer and making one another laugh.

Derek and Vijay got to their new classroom quickly and sat next to each other, before the best seats got taken. They said hi or waved to classmates they already knew, before the bell rang to start the day.

Derek noticed a couple of boys he didn't recognize, sitting together in the back of the classroom. They had to be new to St. Augustine. Otherwise he would have seen them before.

One of the new boys was tall and thin, with an Afro and a Boston Celtics book bag. The other kid was shorter, athletic-looking, with buzz-cut dark hair and brown eyes that darted everywhere, taking in everything.

The two of them were talking a mile a minute, like they were already good friends, so Derek didn't go over and introduce himself.

Across the room, near the window, sat Gary Parnell, Derek's longtime nemesis. Gary shot Derek a half smile and gave a little wave, as if to say, *Here we are again, Jeter*.

Then their new teacher walked in.

Mr. Laithwaite was tall, bald, and a little stooped over. He looked like an eagle sitting high in a tree, waiting for his prey to appear below him.

Mr. Laithwaite had a reputation, too—as the toughest teacher in the entire school.

The whole class hushed immediately. There was something about Mr. Laithwaite that commanded obedience. Derek and Vijay looked at each other, but they didn't dare even whisper, like they would have last year with Ms. Terrapin.

"Class. Welcome. As you may be aware, this is seventh grade. *Not* sixth grade, and *certainly* not kindergarten. I will expect you to behave accordingly."

Yeeesh, thought Derek. It wasn't like anyone was talking or being inattentive.

Mr. Laithwaite's eagle eyes took them in, one by one. "First of all let me hand out these forms, most of which you'll need to show your parents, have them sign, and return to me tomorrow."

The forms were passed out. Derek took one of each and put them into his bag to look over after school.

"This year, as you are aware," Mr. Laithwaite continued, "you will be moving from classroom to classroom for each of your subjects. I will be teaching English and social studies, Ms. Hannigan will be teaching science and math—it's going to be physics and algebra for starters—and Mr. Elder will cover foreign languages."

Algebra . . . physics. . . . Seventh grade sounded more than just hard. It sounded *scary*!

"I will now hand out your schedules," their teacher announced. "If you lose them, don't come to me for a replacement. For that you'll have to visit the dean's office."

Derek squirmed uncomfortably in his seat. Mr. Laithwaite was making it sound like they were in detention camp, not school!

"I am also handing out your first-semester reading list," Mr. Laithwaite said. "And now let me go over your first major assignment for English. We will be practicing public speaking this quarter, and instead of giving individual speeches, we're going to have a series of *debates*—mano a mano, as they say in Spanish." He let out a little laugh, and a few of the students chuckled nervously along with him.

Derek could feel the beads of sweat breaking out on his forehead. Was the air-conditioning broken or something? Or was it just the shadow of a mountain of schoolwork looming over his future?

Public speaking was possibly his least favorite activity in the entire world! He hated being up there in front of everyone with all those eyes on him, waiting for him to say something smart!

Mr. Laithwaite cleared his throat, and the class fell silent again. "Later this week I'm going to pair you up as opponents for each debate. You will choose a topic together, then prepare separately at home, with no further interaction on the project before the actual debate. Each person will have five minutes to argue his or her side, followed by two-minute rebuttals of the other person's argument."

Yikes, thought Derek. It was bad enough reading a prepared speech in front of everyone. But rebuttals meant speaking off the cuff—without a script! That was even scarier!

"We will conclude with a thirty-second final statement by each side," the teacher went on. "The class will then vote on the winner. That is to say, they will not vote on which side of the argument they agree with but on who made the best case. Debates will begin at the end of this month, and we'll do two or three each day until we're done—so you'll have plenty of time to prepare, class."

The rest of the day went by in a blur. Each of Derek's new

teachers handed out forms and textbooks and outlined the work the class would be doing. But Derek couldn't get his mind off the idea of being in front of everyone, making a fool of himself. Just imagining it was sheer torture.

By the time the final bell rang, Derek knew for sure that this was going to be a tough year academically in more ways than that. He hoisted his now-heavy book bag, closed his empty locker, and headed for the school bus.

"Derek!"

Derek swung around to find Mr. Nelson, the school's basketball coach, approaching him. "Hi, Coach!"

"You ready for a big season, kid?"

"Totally—ready for tryouts tomorrow!"

"No need for that. Tryouts are for the kids I haven't seen in action." Derek had played for Coach Nelson the previous season in the AAU league. "As far as I'm concerned, you're already on the team. Just bring the effort and type of play you showed last year, and I'll see you at first practice."

"Really?"

"Listen, you were a super-sub last year, so in my mind you're ready for a starting position. Of course, we'll see who shows up at tryouts—maybe Michael Jordan." He laughed. "Seriously, though. I'm counting on you to be a team leader."

"Me?"

"I don't know why that surprises you. The Friars missed

the playoffs last year, and I was kind of counting on Dave Hennum at center to carry a big part of the load this season. But he's gone, and our all-star forward transferred to public school. You've got as much experience as anyone else who's trying out for the team. I'm counting on you to set an example. Understood?"

"Got it, Coach."

"Good. See you at first practice."

He left Derek standing there, deep in thought. Derek liked the idea of being a team leader, for sure. It didn't scare him. After all, he'd been a leader on most of his baseball teams.

He headed to the school bus, excited now for the coming season. Of course, schoolwork would be tougher than it had ever been. He'd be putting in longer hours of homework and studying. Practices took time too. And there would be pressure on him to perform, both in academics and in basketball.

But Derek wasn't about to let that stop him. He'd handled plenty of pressure last spring, with baseball playoffs, finals, and more, hadn't he?

Sure, it would be even harder this time around. But he'd learned how to deal with the challenge while making sure he had fun along the way, reminding himself often why he was working so hard in the first place.

He knew good grades were vital for his future. And as far as basketball went, his competitive nature would carry him through. He rode home on the bus, feeling confident that he could handle whatever came his way.

Except for one thing—*debating in front of the whole class.*

"I hate second grade!"

As soon as he came in the door, Derek heard Sharlee's raised voice coming from the kitchen. He found her sitting at the table opposite their dad, her papers and pencils laid out in front of her.

"My first day of school, and I already have to do *homework*!" she moaned, appealing to Derek with upturned palms, as if to say, *Can you believe this nonsense?*

"Now, come on, Sharlee," said Mr. Jeter. "It's only a few examples. You know how to do it. Just take ten minutes, and you'll be done before you know it."

"But it's so *unfair*! My teacher says we're going to get homework *every . . . single . . . day*!"

Derek suppressed a chuckle. "Welcome to the world of the big kids," he said. "I guess you really are almost a grown-up by now, huh?"

Sharlee paused, thinking about it. "Well . . . that's true. But it's not worth it if I have to do homework *every day*!"

"It's not like you have a choice," Mr. Jeter said. "You're growing up whether you like it or not."

"Well, I *don't* like it!" Sharlee said, crossing her arms and nodding, as if that were the final word.

"You don't have to like homework," Derek told her. "I get that, totally. But it goes a lot more easily if you find something to enjoy about it."

"Now, *those* are some wise words, Derek," his dad said. "Speaking of which, have *you* got any homework today?"

"Not yet. Just this load of forms and announcements to go through."

"That doesn't count as homework!" Sharlee objected. "I have those too!"

"Okay, okay," Derek said. "You win the who-got-the-most-homework contest, at least for today. Meanwhile, let me get through all this."

He sat down between the two of them and opened his book bag. There were permission forms for class trips and other activities, like the ropes course in the gym. He looked each of the forms over, then put them into a pile for his mom and dad to look at.

There were announcements about events and fund-raising projects too. Derek opened up his monthly calendar and entered all the dates, just the way Mr. Laithwaite had instructed them to do.

And then Derek saw it, one last announcement, from the Kalamazoo County Recreation Department: TRYOUTS FOR BASEBALL TRAVEL TEAMS!

Derek read further. There were teams for different age groups, from eleven years old on up, each with openings at multiple positions.

Derek remembered meeting the travel team's coach way back in June. Mr. Russell had introduced himself to Derek after a ball game, saying he admired the way Derek played shortstop, praising his dedication, and inviting him to try out at shortstop in the fall.

At the time it had seemed to Derek like the coach was saying, "If you try out, you're going to make it." But now, months later, he wasn't so sure. Had the coach really meant it that way?

Derek knew there would be other kids trying out for the position—talented kids. But the coach's words kept ringing in his ears. . . . "I like the way you play the game, kid."

One thing was for sure—he was going to try out. Even though he was already trying out for the basketball team, he couldn't let a chance like this go by, could he?

In fact, the idea of being on *both* teams, of playing two sports at once, sounded supercool!

The form said that in the fall session, travel baseball was mostly practices and instruction, with a few local games sprinkled here and there. It was a way for players to keep working on their skills until the main season, in spring and summer.

Derek was psyched about the instructional part. He knew he needed to become a better player if he wanted to make it all the way to the Yankees someday.

But the main reason for trying out *now* was that the fall

team *stayed together* for next year's spring and summer season. If he made the team now, he'd get to play all next year with—and against—some of the best players in the whole state!

Derek let himself imagine being on both teams for a moment—basketball and travel baseball. Then he remembered that schoolwork wasn't going to disappear while all this was going on.

Maybe I'm trying to do too much?

He asked himself the question, then immediately put it out of his mind.

No way, he thought. *I've got to figure out how to fit it all in. It's too big an opportunity to miss!*

Chapter Three

BACK ON THE HILL

Mr. Jeter finished grading the last of his papers and stacked them together. Then his gaze fell on Derek's pile of forms. "Are all those for me to look at?"

"Uh . . . yeah," Derek answered, sliding the pile over. He held on to the travel team announcement, though.

Way back in June, Derek's parents had been generally supportive about Derek trying out come September. But he'd never actually *asked* their permission. Autumn had seemed a long way off back then, and he'd figured he would ask them when the time was right.

But now that tryouts were only three days away, Derek was reminded of the fact that he would need his parents' permission, which was not going to be a slam dunk at all.

Travel baseball was expensive. It also took up a lot of time, and one of his parents would sometimes have to get up super-early to drive him up to an hour each way for games.

On top of that, Derek was confident he would make the basketball team—*and* was about to be buried in schoolwork. His parents had always supported his baseball dream of playing for the Yankees, but they were also laser-focused on his grades.

Derek figured there was about a fifty-fifty shot that his parents would let him try out for the travel team. Which meant he needed to find the right approach, and the perfect time to ask.

Which was definitely not now.

Derek had no idea yet how to ask so that he got a yes in response. And anyway, his mom needed to be part of the conversation, and she wasn't home yet.

"What about *that* form?" his dad asked, nodding toward the paper Derek still had clutched in his hands. "Do I need to see that, too?"

"Oh. This one? Um, I'll show you later, okay? When Mom's here. Meanwhile, can I go over to the Hill for a while?"

"Well, all right. But be back before six. Mom's going to be hungry when she gets home."

Derek went upstairs, dropped the book bag, got his mitt and bat, and ran back downstairs. "See you guys at six!" he called out as he left.

"It's not fair!" he heard Sharlee shout behind him. "Daddy, why are you letting *him* go play while *I* have to sit here and do homework?"

Derek shut the door behind him before his dad had a chance to change his mind. *Sharlee really is growing up,* he thought, jogging toward the sloping patch of grass the kids had named Jeter's Hill—because he was always there, playing baseball with whoever showed up.

He thought again about the travel team flyer. Tryouts were this Saturday—just three days away!

Derek felt a sudden wave of worry go through him. He hadn't played serious baseball all summer, except for those two games with the city kids. Most of the time he'd just thrown the ball around with his cousins on the big lawn. He hadn't even been to the batting cages—not once!

He was sure all the other kids trying out had been hitting in the cages all summer. And probably getting private coaching, too! Meanwhile he had only three days to get his game into tip-top shape!

He knew his family would go out to practice with him once or twice before then—but would that be enough?

He sure hoped the other kids would be on the Hill, waiting for him. . . .

"There he is! I told you he'd be here!"

Derek heard Vijay's voice ring out from the Hill even before he spotted him. But whom was he talking to?

It was *Avery*!

Avery, who'd become one of their crew last spring, when she'd been the only girl on Derek and Vijay's Little League team.

She and her friends—most of them older—lived about half a mile away. They'd temporarily lost their ball field to renovations, so they'd started coming to the Hill instead, which in Derek's humble opinion made playing there more fun, and more competitive.

"Long time, no see!" She greeted Derek with double high fives. "Feels like years."

"Hey, it's only been, what, eight weeks? Nine?"

"Well, I'm sure you were having a blast in New Jersey or wherever, so it probably went by in a blink," she said. "Back here things were kind of slow."

"Avery's right," Vijay agreed. "Lots of kids were away at summer camp or vacationing with their parents. We never had enough players to put together a decent game."

"Huh," said Derek, looking around. "Looks like they still haven't come back. We're the only ones here, and it's already five o'clock."

"'Cause it's the first day of school," Avery said. "All my friends are in eighth grade or high school, and they've got, like, zero time. Work up to here." She motioned to her neck.

"I know the feeling," Derek said. "But never mind. How 'bout we do some fungoes? I've got travel team tryouts on Saturday, and I haven't thrown or hit for weeks!"

They rotated between first base, shortstop, and batter. Derek started at the "plate," which was just a flat rock, really. Five minutes in he could see that Vijay's fielding had really improved. Derek guessed that Avery had been working with him over the summer, giving him pointers.

Her game was even better than Derek remembered. She speared balls, dived and leapt to make spectacular catches, and snared difficult short hops, one after another.

"You know," he told her when she came in to take her turn hitting, "you really ought to consider trying out."

"What, for the travel team?" she asked. "Nah. No way."

"Why not? You're plenty good enough, and I'll bet there's an opening at second base. We could be the double-play combination, just like last spring!"

She was looking down at the ground now. "I already asked my mom, and she said no."

Derek was silent for a moment. "Oh. I see."

"She said we can't afford it. There's all the fees for uniforms and stuff, and I'd need new cleats and a better mitt. Plus, she isn't wild about me going all over the place with a bunch of boys, even if it is to play ball."

Derek didn't say anything. He could tell that Avery wasn't done explaining.

"Hey, are we playing or not?" Vijay called from second base, where he'd shifted over to, opening shortstop for Derek.

"Hold up a minute," Derek told him, raising his palm. To Avery he said, "You were saying?"

She swallowed hard, and Derek could tell she was really bummed out. "My mom says the boys on the travel team are so competitive that they won't be cool about it if I make an error, or if I strike out in the clutch or something. She said it's different from in Little League—that if a girl messes up, they won't treat her the same as if a boy does."

"Hey," Derek said, "it happened in Little League too, and you never let it stop you then."

She shrugged, reaching for the bat he was holding. He gave it to her, grabbed his mitt, and started out to short-stop. "Well, I hope your mom changes her mind," he called to her as he went.

As he stood out there, taking grounders and line drives, Derek felt bad for Avery. He was sure it was money that had made her mom say no. Anyone who knew Avery knew she could handle herself on a team of competitive boys.

He couldn't help wondering what sacrifices his own parents would have to make to cover the expenses of travel baseball. They weren't exactly millionaires, he knew, and they worked hard for every penny they earned. Would they allow him to sign up for such an expensive activity?

Hmm. . . . Maybe if I did extra chores . . . ?

But with all the schoolwork his teachers were already piling on, and with Coach Nelson counting on him to help lead the basketball team, where would he be able to find time for extra chores?

Luckily, Harry Hicks, Jeff Jacobson, and a couple of other kids showed up just then, and Derek had no time to think any further about it.

"I'm trying out too!" Harry said when Derek told him about his plans. "Pitcher—that's my spot. I've got dibs on it!"

Soon they were all playing ball, and Derek reveled in the familiar sounds and rhythms of the game he loved. Glancing over at Avery, he saw that it was the same for her. While the game was on, nothing else mattered—the whole world disappeared. . . .

Until he glanced at his watch and saw that it was 5:55.

"Gotta fly, guys. See you next time!" he said with a wave, before starting home, running full tilt to make sure he didn't show up late. He didn't want his parents already mad at him when he was about to ask them for the biggest favor ever!

Chapter Four

THE BIG ASK

As the Jeter family sat down to dinner, Derek was already anxious. He wished he could try out for the team first, *then* ask their permission *if* he made the team.

But that wasn't how the Jeter family worked. Besides, the tryouts were at Westwood Fields, so Derek would need a ride there and back.

He sat at the table, waiting for the right moment to bring up the subject. But it wasn't easy, because Sharlee was taking up all of Mom's and Dad's attention, by asking for something *very similar*.

"Why can't I play soccer *and* do acrobatics?" she complained. "It's not fair! Ciara is doing both, so why can't I?"

"We didn't say you couldn't," said Mrs. Jeter. "We only said it was a lot to take on."

"It *isn't*!" Sharlee insisted. "Soccer is on Saturday mornings, and acro is on Thursdays after school!"

"Hmm . . . ," their mom said, looking over at her husband. "Jeter? What do you think?"

Mr. Jeter put down his fork and knife and looked at Sharlee. "You really are into acrobatics, aren't you? I've seen you doing all those cartwheels and handstands in the living room. And you didn't bang into the furniture even once. . . . And I know how you love soccer. . . ." He looked at his wife. "What do you say, Dot?"

"Can you get her there and back on Thursdays, Jeter? I've got work."

"Thursday is my early day. . . . Sure, I'll do it, if you'll take her to soccer on Saturdays."

"YAY!" Sharlee yelled, clapping. "Woo-hoo! I have the best parents ever!"

Derek cleared his throat. *"Hm-hmm!"*

Everyone looked at him. "Derek?" his mom said.

"I also, um, have a request," he said, not sure how to put it.

"Well?" His dad was looking at him, waiting for more.

"Um, I'd like to try out for the . . . um . . . travel baseball team?"

"*And* play basketball?" his mom asked, taken aback.

"I can do it, Mom!" Derek pleaded, heading her off before she could say no. "I checked both calendars, and fall baseball is mostly just practices and instruction, with a game or two thrown in, but if I don't get on that team now, I won't be eligible for all of next year!"

"Hmm," said his dad. "I see where you're coming from, Derek. Still, travel ball takes a big chunk of time."

"Not to mention money!" said his mom.

"It's twice a week, and so is basketball. I can handle it all! Really!"

"I don't know, Derek. . . . Your mom is right. Travel ball is expensive."

"There are no expenses in fall, Dad, because the team doesn't travel anywhere—only equipment and fees and stuff."

"Equipment and fees aren't free either," his mom said.

"Mom, Dad, you said you'd back me all the way if I honored my contract."

"And we meant it," said Mrs. Jeter. "But the contract also says you've got to keep up with your schoolwork, which comes first, before sports or any other activities."

"You're letting *Sharlee* do two things," Derek pointed out.

"Sharlee's in second grade. You're in seventh," said Mr. Jeter. "You've got a lot more on your plate, when you add it all up."

Then Sharlee suddenly piped up. "But we *both* get homework every day, so you should let Derek do two things too!"

Derek smiled. "Thanks, Sharlee."

"Don't mention it." Sharlee nodded emphatically and

crossed her arms, as if to say, *Go argue with* that!

"I assume you have a plan for how to handle everything?" Mr. Jeter asked.

"I do," Derek answered. "And as far as the cost, I'm ready to put in all my birthday money. Plus I'll do extra chores. I promise! Please?"

"I don't see how you'll have time to fit in extra chores," his mom said dubiously.

"Mom, this could be a huge step for me!" Derek pleaded, finally getting down to the heart of the matter. "How's my big dream ever going to come true if I don't go for every opportunity when it appears?"

There was a long moment of silence. Derek saw his parents giving each other meaningful looks, communicating everything without words.

Finally his dad said, "Derek, I want you to understand something, before we agree to *anything. . . .*"

Derek felt a thrill go through him. *They were going to say yes!*

"There are a lot of ifs that go along with this, son. But *if* the coach is flexible about conflicts with school and basketball, and *if* you keep abiding by all the clauses in your contract—*including* keeping up your grades . . ."

"*If* you do all that," Mrs. Jeter said, "we'll put in whatever money your contribution doesn't cover. We'll dispense with the extra chores this time, in light of everything else you're doing."

"Thanks, Mom and Dad! This is awesome!" Derek grinned. "I have the best parents ever!"

"How about *me*?" Sharlee protested. "I helped you convince them, didn't I?"

"You did!" Derek admitted. "Thanks, Sharlee. You're the best *sister* ever. I really, *really* appreciate it!"

"You *should*," she said matter-of-factly.

"Wow!" Derek said. "I can't believe this is happening!"

Now all he had to do was *make the team*.

Chapter Five

THE GATHERING STORM

"Class. Your attention, please."

It had been only a few days, but everyone already knew how it worked with Mr. Laithwaite. First he called for quiet in his nice, calm voice. If that didn't work, he went straight to the whistle. It hung around his neck and had a piercing sound that, apparently, only Mr. Laithwaite could stand.

After three days the whistle was no longer needed. Everyone hushed instantly at the sound of their teacher's voice.

And it wasn't just the whistle. Something *else* about Mr. Laithwaite had them all off balance. Even the usual class clowns had fallen into line. Derek had never been in a room this quiet—not even the library!

"It's time to start our debating unit," the teacher said. "You'll be paired up, you'll take opposite sides of a proposition of your choosing, and after the debate the class will vote on who won. Clear?"

"Yes, sir," everyone said in unison.

Derek winced at the thought of being up there talking, with the whole class watching, and literally judging him! The last time he'd had to do public speaking, it had been for a science project, where he'd been paired with Gary, of all people.

It had gone okay in the end, and they'd each gotten a good grade, but the whole experience had been . . . unpleasant, to say the least.

"I've got all your names in here," said Mr. Laithwaite, mixing around folded bits of paper in a metal bowl. He drew out two. "Marissa . . . and Melvin."

Marissa and Melvin waved to each other from across the room, smiling as if they'd been paired up for a dance.

Derek hoped he'd be paired with someone nice and not too argumentative. *Vijay*, he thought, would be the perfect opponent. He would definitely out-argue Derek, but at least it would be less of an ordeal.

But no. Vijay's partner was one of the two new boys, Marcus Baines—the tall one, with an Afro that made him look even taller.

"Gary Parnell," Mr. Laithwaite intoned. Derek held his breath. And then Mr. Laithwaite said, "And . . . Derek Jeter."

Noooooooooo!

Derek buried his face in his hands. When he looked up again and glanced over at Gary, his designated opponent was wearing a smug, satisfied grin.

Derek swung back around to face the teacher, barely listening as the other kids were paired up. All he knew was, he was already the unluckiest kid in Kalamazoo.

Gary was not only the smartest kid in the class, scoring the highest grades almost every time, but he also *loved* to torment Derek, who had had the nerve to occasionally score higher. In Gary's mind, showing Derek up with the whole class watching would be pretty close to heaven.

Derek could picture it now—Gary slicing through his arguments with those snide, "humorous" digs of his. . . .

This was going to be *awful*. Derek was sure of it. At least last time they'd been on the same side. This time they'd be facing off against each other. And having been paired with Derek once already, Gary was well aware of Derek's terror of public speaking. He was sure to take advantage, messing with Derek's mind every chance he got!

"All right," said Mr. Laithwaite. "You all now have fifteen minutes to meet with your partners and choose a topic for debate. I have written some suggestions on the blackboard, and you're free to choose one of them."

Gary sat at his desk, leaning back with his hands clasped behind his head, legs stretched out in front of him, and still wearing the same contented grin.

Derek got up and went over to him, because time was passing, and he knew Gary would never get up and come over to *his* desk.

"Well, Jeter, here we go again!" Gary said cheerfully. "It must be fate—or, in your case, doom."

"Very funny," Derek shot back glumly. "About as funny as Mr. Laithwaite."

Gary laughed. "Good one, Jeter. Glad to see you haven't lost *your* sense of humor. You're going to need it this time."

"I always do, when it comes to you."

"Oooo, I'm wounded. *Not.* So . . . anything you'd particularly like to argue about? I'm wide open."

"What I'd really like is to not have to do this."

"Aww, my heart bleeds. Any of the options strike your fancy? I'll let you pick. It's the least I can do, considering what you're about to go through."

Derek ignored the dig and took a look at the topics on offer. Most of them didn't appeal, except the one that read "Resolved: the driving age should be raised to 19."

Derek was about to suggest it, when Marcus walked up to the blackboard and erased it, meaning he was choosing it for his debate with Vijay.

Oh, well. "I guess we should just pick a topic of our own," Derek said.

"As in . . . ?"

"I don't know, Gary!" Derek said, annoyed. "I don't even want to be *doing* this! I've got a million other things on my mind."

"Such as?"

"You really want to know?"

"Sure. I'm in a generous mood, Jeter. Babble on."

"So, I'm going to be on the basketball team. And I'm also trying out for travel baseball—which, if I make the team, means I've got a crammed schedule."

Gary shook his head, perplexed. "I don't get you, Jeter. One sport at a time is not enough for you? Have you lost what little is left of your mind?"

Derek smiled. "Nope. And why should I give up either sport? Baseball's great, and so is basketball!"

Now it was Gary's turn to grin. "Jeter, you just gave us our debate topic!"

"Huh?"

"Resolved: schools should cut back on sports teams and activities, and concentrate solely on academics."

"That's crazy," Derek said.

"I knew you'd say that," Gary commented, sneering. "Which is what makes it the perfect thing for us to debate. So naturally I'll be pro, and you'll be con."

"You know what, Gary? That's brilliant."

"I want that in writing, Jeter," Gary joked.

"It's brilliant because there's no way you can defend it."

"Oh yeah? Watch me." Gary smirked. "And you can go ahead and thank me, Jeter. I'm giving you a gift, the rare topic you actually know something about."

"I'm moved by your generosity, Gary. Really. Thank you."

"Well, you're a busy man—kind of like a hamster on its wheel, huh? I don't want to waste your precious time unnecessarily."

Derek was about to offer another comeback when Mr. Laithwaite's quiet voice interrupted, saying their fifteen minutes was up.

Derek went back to his seat, feeling unsettled. Why had Gary offered to make sports the topic? Surely not to make it easier for Derek. Gary wasn't that charitable, even in his best mood.

Then it hit him. Gary had suggested "Ban all sports teams" because he was sure he would win the debate!

Well, not so fast, thought Derek. Sometimes people "knew" things that turned out to be wrong. Most kids enjoyed sports. Even if Gary was the best debater in the world, Derek felt sure he had a chance to win. He still had to deal with his own terrors, of course, but at least now he had a reason to face his fears. He was going into battle over something he really believed in!

"Hey, Derek!"

"Vij! Hey!" Derek greeted his pal with a fist bump as he stood at his locker.

"See you on the Hill later?"

"Uh, no. I've got basketball practice today."

"Oh. Cool. I forgot you were on the school team this year. So . . . tomorrow, then?"

Derek shook his head. "Travel team tryouts."

"Wow. Busy guy. Sunday, then, I guess." Vijay seemed suddenly deflated.

Derek could tell that his friend was disappointed. "Sorry, Vij. It's just . . . I've got a lot going on this week. We'll find time, though."

"For sure," Vijay said, not sounding totally convinced. "Okay, see you Monday in class."

"Definitely."

After his friend had gone, Derek headed for the boys' locker room, next to the gym. When he got there, half the team was already getting suited up. Derek was excited to see who'd made the squad.

He already knew Sam Rockman would be there. Sam greeted him with a high five. "Hey, hey, Derek! You good to go?"

"We got this, Sam," Derek replied confidently, high-fiving him. "Just like in AAU last year."

Coach Nelson handed them shiny purple uniforms, and the boys changed into them. Derek had number 1, for starting point guard. Sam had number 2—shooting guard.

Derek already knew the two kids who wore 3 and 4— the starting forwards, Jose Quintana and Tyquan Reeves. Derek had seen them play and knew they were good rebounders and strong finishers in the paint. Tyquan could also sink long and midrange jumpers pretty consistently—a good teammate to dish it to if you got double-teamed.

Derek recognized the tall kid wearing number 5, the starting center, from Mr. Laithwaite's class—Marcus.

And there was Marcus's friend, too, with his buzz-cut dark hair and that intense look in his brown eyes. Gio Milano was his name, and he was wearing number 6. Derek figured that meant he was the second-string point guard—Derek's sub.

Just then Gio gave Derek a sharp look in return, almost staring at him. Derek wondered what that look meant.

It wasn't friendly, whatever it was.

Derek looked back at Marcus. He looked like he could play, all right. Still, Derek wished it were his old pal Dave wearing number 5, and that they could have vied for a championship together. Seeing Marcus wearing Dave's number brought the pain of loss right back.

Once the team got onto the court, though, Derek was able to put all such thoughts behind him. He concentrated on each drill and exercise, putting everything he had into it.

He also got a look at how the rest of the players approached things. He saw, for instance, how Marcus and Gio favored each other when it was time for pass-arounds. They hardly passed the ball to anyone else!

They also took every minute between drills to clown around with each other, telling goofy jokes and cracking up at the weird faces they made.

Derek wondered if Coach Nelson noticed. He seemed

taken up with running the practice and not too concerned with what was going on in between drills.

Derek understood. There'd be time for talking discipline later on. For now the coach, like Derek, wanted to see what the team's makeup was, take its temperature, and get a sense of its strengths and weaknesses.

Derek had to admit that both Gio and Marcus were good players. Marcus was a very athletic center, taller than Dave by a good three inches. He could block a shot, grab a rebound, and even dunk with style. And Gio had real playground skills, ballhandling like a Harlem Globetrotter and making circus-like layups and no-look passes with ease and flair.

In fact, Derek could see the Friars being a big winner this season, if they learned to play together as a unit. But he knew that was easier said than done.

A couple of times during practice, when Coach praised him for putting out extra effort, Derek caught Marcus and Gio looking at him and whispering to each other.

He could tell that whatever they were saying wasn't flattering. Reading lips, he thought Gio was saying, "Coach's pet." But he couldn't be sure.

Derek tried not to let on that he'd noticed. He knew it was best for the team if he just set an example of hard work and let the rest sort itself out.

Marcus and Gio didn't have to like him, so long as they came to respect him, and the effort he gave every time he was on the floor. But all practice long, Derek could feel Gio's dark eyes boring right through him. That kid *wanted* something, and Derek could already sense what it was—the job of starting point guard.

Derek's job.

Chapter Six

TRIAL AND TRIUMPH

Sitting in the back seat of the family's old station wagon, Derek was as jumpy as a cricket. He kept tugging at the leather laces on his mitt, making sure they wouldn't come loose while he was in the middle of his big tryout.

He'd played it over and over in his mind a hundred times—the conversation he'd had with Coach Russell back in late June . . . the coach inviting him to try out. At the time it had seemed like a definite thing—if Derek tried out, he'd make the team.

But now, more than two months later, it didn't seem like such a done deal, especially once they pulled up at Westwood Fields and Derek saw the crowd of kids who'd shown up to try out.

Derek knew there were a lot of holdovers from last year's eleven-and-up team. It would be hard to crack the established lineup and win a spot on the team.

His mom parked the car, and with Sharlee in tow they walked toward the stands, which were filled with kids and their families.

"Don't worry," said Mrs. Jeter. "Sharlee and I will find someplace to sit. You go ahead and tell the coaches you're here." She kissed him on the cheek and clapped him on the shoulder. "Go get 'em, old man."

"You can do it, Derek!" Sharlee said, reaching her arms around him. "You're the best player in Kalamazoo!"

Derek had to laugh. "Thanks, sis," he said. "You and Vijay have me rated a notch above Babe Ruth."

He left them there and jogged over to home plate, where Coach Russell was standing, holding a sheaf of papers and pens and handing them to kids to fill out.

"Hey, buddy," he greeted Derek. "Glad you came down. Here you go." He handed Derek a paper and a pen, but to Derek it was as if he'd been given the keys to the kingdom.

The coach remembered him! At least it sounded like he did. . . .

Once everyone had finished their forms, all three coaches stood on the mound, with the players around them in a circle.

"Welcome, everyone, and thanks for coming down to try out. My name is Rick Russell, and I'm the head coach.

These are my assistants, Joe Mendoza and Richie Bern-stein. Both of them have professional baseball experience. I only played college ball myself, but I've been coaching for ten years—the last five of them, travel ball.

"Well, that's enough about us. We're here today to learn about *you*. Now, we only have three slots open. But we will take on one additional alternate, someone who can play in case one of the other players is sick or injured.

"Now I want to form you up into three groups—one for each coach, so we each get a look at you. You'll be doing hitting and baserunning with me, fielding with Coach Joe, and pitching with Coach Richie. Afterward we'll have one last drill where we put it all together, so we can see you in simulated game action. Understood?"

"Yes, Coach!" everyone yelled in unison.

Derek was impressed. He *always* responded like that— but in Little League the coach usually had to ask at least twice to get a loud enough response.

Not here, though. Every one of these kids was really into baseball. *Just like him.*

He remembered back to when he was in second grade and his teacher had the kids write about what they wanted to be when they grew up. Derek had written about want-ing to be the Yankees' shortstop someday, and she'd given him a bad grade, because she'd said it was "unrealistic."

Derek's parents hadn't liked that one bit. They'd let the teacher know, in no uncertain terms, that they were committed to supporting his dream and helping him achieve it.

Derek had taken heart from their support. They believed in him, so how could he not believe in himself?

Did all these kids here today feel the same way? They sure acted like it. Derek realized they all must have been among the best players on their Little League teams, year after year. It made him understand something he hadn't quite realized before today:

There was nothing all that special about anything he'd done in baseball so far!

Then again, that was why he was here—to take the next giant step toward achieving his big dream.

Once drills got started, Derek gradually began to relax. Among the kids trying out, none seemed to have better fielding skills than he did.

At the plate, Derek had a really good session too, even hitting a pair of long balls that would have been dingers in any Little League game.

While he was waiting his turn for each drill, he glanced over to second base. A lot of the kids there seemed to be having trouble handling tough grounders, including bunts.

Derek wished Avery were here. She was definitely a cut above any one of them. She would have made the team for sure!

At the end of drills, Derek went over to Harry to say hello. "How's it going for you, Har?"

"So-so," Harry said, slightly downcast. "My changeup was okay, and I had good pop on my fastball, but I was all over the place. I guess I was too hyped up about today."

Derek had known Harry a long time. He tended to be negative about most things. He'd once thrown cold water onto Derek's dream of being a Yankee too.

"You know you always see the glass as half-empty, Harry. I'll bet you make the team anyway."

"Hope so," Harry said. "You too."

"Thanks. See you in uniform, then." At least that got a smile out of Harry.

The final drill was unusual. The pitchers were told to throw low in the strike zone—fastballs only. The hitters were instructed to try to make solid contact, rather than trying to hit homers with every swing. Hitters got three swings each, then ran the bases until they were either tagged out or made it home safely. Then the groups rotated.

By the end of the tryout, Derek was satisfied that he'd given it everything he had. He hadn't made a single error in the field, and he'd had one of his best days behind the plate.

True, the other kids trying out at short turned out to be better than he'd first thought. But he still felt fairly optimistic about making the team.

He also felt *bone-tired*. After the previous day's basketball practice and today's three-hour marathon tryout, going full throttle every minute, he was just plain beat. "Let's go home," he told his mom and Sharlee.

"You did great, Derek!" Sharlee told him. "I saw you hit those homers. You *are* better than Babe Ruth!"

"Sharlee, cut it out. You'll jinx me."

"I should call you Baby Ruth, like the candy bar."

"You'd better not. Seriously. *No.*"

Sharlee giggled. "Okay, okay. But you've got to admit it's funny."

Derek rolled his eyes.

"I'm sure your dad is just bursting with curiosity to hear how it went," said Mrs. Jeter. "He would have loved being here, but—"

"I know, I know," Derek said. "Work, work, work."

"Hey, you've been working pretty hard yourself, old man. Not that that's a *bad* thing."

Not unless you're working on having a debate with Gary, Derek thought.

Everything hurt. Derek kept shifting around on the couch trying to get comfortable. In one position his knees ached. In another it was his middle back. He let out the occasional groan as he moved, and that got his dad's attention.

"You sound like an old grandpa." Mr. Jeter turned down the volume on the TV, where the Tigers were losing yet another crucial late-season game.

"I overdid it the last couple of days," Derek admitted. "I'm stiff and sore all over."

"Got to pace yourself. Look what happened to Carsten."

Derek rolled his eyes. "What was I supposed to do, Dad? It was the first basketball practice, and it was tryouts for travel team! I *had* to give it everything."

"Okay, that's true. I guess I'm all worked up about the Tigers. . . ."

When the family had moved to Kalamazoo, way back when Derek had been four years old, his dad had adopted his new state's team, and he'd been a rabid Tigers fan ever since.

Derek, on the other hand, had never changed his allegiance from the Yankees. He and his grandma back in New Jersey were now the family's biggest Yankees fans.

"If Carsten had let the manager sit him down back in August, when he'd first tweaked his hamstring, he'd be back in the lineup right now, and we'd be scoring twice as many runs. That's my point."

"Well, *I can't* sit myself down, Dad. Coach Nelson told me straight up he was counting on me to be a team leader."

"Really? I'm happy to hear that, Derek. It makes me proud. But remember, you've got to work smart, not just hard. Carsten should have sat himself down if he wasn't right."

"But the team's counting on him, Dad!"

"I get that, Derek. But he *can't* be counted on to

contribute on the field now, can he? Not for at least two weeks, and there's only four weeks left in the season! He'll need to lead from the bench during that time. We've got six games to make up on Boston, and we're only scoring two runs per game without Carsten in the lineup."

The phone rang, interrupting them. "I'll get it!" Derek said, bounding off the couch.

"Wow," his dad said, watching him run for the kitchen. "You sure recovered fast. I wish Carsten could bounce back like that!"

It was true. In his excitement Derek had totally forgotten about his aching body. He'd been waiting for that phone to ring ever since he'd gotten home from tryouts.

"Hello?"

"Derek? It's Coach Russell."

"Yes! Hi!"

"I'm, uh, calling to say you made the team."

"YESSSSS!" Derek yelled, pumping his fist.

"You were outstanding at tryouts, Derek. I'm looking forward to working with you on the finer points of your game—if you say yes, of course."

Derek looked over his shoulder. Mr. Jeter had come into the kitchen, obviously alerted by Derek's joyful shout.

"Of course! Thank you, Coach!"

"Great! Great. Can you put your parents on? I'll need to go over things with them first and get their okay."

"You, uh, you want to talk to my dad? He's right here."

Mr. Jeter took the receiver and said hello, then listened as the coach laid things out. ". . . Mm-hm. . . . Well, thank you. He's a good boy. We're very proud of him. . . . Well . . . Hmm. . . . I see. . . ."

It went on and on, and Derek thought he'd burst from the suspense. His dad's face didn't give much away about whether he was going to agree or not. And the more the coach spoke, the more serious Mr. Jeter's face became.

Derek's mom walked in, saying, "Okay, Sharlee's in bed—oh! Sorry." She put a finger to her lips and sat down next to Derek at the kitchen table.

Mr. Jeter was practically frowning now. Derek sat forward on the edge of his seat. "I do want to talk with you about Derek's other commitments," Derek's dad said into the phone.

Derek swallowed hard. His dad was laying it all out, about the basketball team, about Derek's commitment to keeping up his grades, even about his contract!

Then Mr. Jeter fell silent, listening to the coach's response. "Mm-hm. . . . Right. . . . I see. . . ."

Derek felt like he was about to burst. He had to know what the coach was saying!

"Well," his dad said, "we've had that conversation with him, and he knows he has to balance everything and manage his time and energy. So if you're comfortable with it, we're on board."

Derek's eyes widened and his jaw dropped. Was his dream actually about to come true?

"All right, then," said his dad. "Nice talking to you, Coach. I'll just have to run it by my wife, but I don't think she'll object. We've been over this together, so . . . Right. I will. Bye."

He hung up the phone and turned to Derek. "He said it shouldn't be a problem, since this is fall season and mostly practice and instruction, and not a lot of games." He turned to his wife. "What do you think, Dot? Derek says Coach Nelson is counting on him to be a team leader. You don't think it'll be taking on too much?"

She shrugged. "As long as Derek can handle the load, I think it's great."

"Thanks, Mom!" Derek said, hugging her, then throwing his arms around his father, too. "Thanks, Dad!"

"Congratulations, Derek," said Mr. Jeter.

"This is a big step for you, old man," said his mom, flashing a big smile.

His dad took him by the shoulders and looked him up and down. "You know what?" he said. "I think you grew a couple of inches over the summer. Going to be tall after all, huh?"

That night Derek had a hard time going to sleep. He was just too excited and happy to settle down. Finally he gave up, turned the light back on, and opened up his calendar. Date by date he started to pencil in the schedule of basketball practices and games. It worked out to about one practice and one game per week.

When he was done with that, Derek added in twice-weekly baseball practices. Then he flipped through the weeks between now and November 1, when travel team ended until spring.

His calendar was already crammed. And by the time he'd filled in the blocks for homework and studying, there were barely any open time slots left!

Exhausted just thinking about it, Derek yawned, shut off the light, and got back into bed.

It's going to be a crazy couple of months, he realized as he nodded off. And there was one thing there wasn't going to be any time for at all—

Playing ball on the Hill.

Chapter Seven

BE A LEADER

Gio was seething. Derek could tell. The steam was practically coming out of the kid's ears, and he was looking daggers right at Derek.

Coach Nelson had just read out the starting lineup for the Friars' first game, and he'd named Derek as starting point guard. Derek was excited to be named the starter, but not surprised.

But the news obviously came as a shock to Gio, who had dazzled everyone with his moves and hustle at the team's first practice. He'd obviously thought he'd made enough of an impression to get the job over Derek (who'd also had a good practice, if less flashy).

Marcus was starting at center. No surprise there, either,

in Dave's absence. But it must have galled Gio even more that his friend was starting and he wasn't.

Derek decided to ignore their dirty looks and concentrate on getting the Friars out to an early lead against their opponents—the Padres of Saint Francis, from clear across town.

From the Friars' first possession, Derek was determined to spread the ball around, especially to the team's shooters—Sam, at shooting guard, and Tyquan, their small forward. Both were deadly accurate from midrange—*usually*. But whether it was nerves or adrenaline, or whatever, they started out the game ice-cold, even though Derek was finding his teammates with passes for open looks at the basket.

Meanwhile the Padres were grabbing every rebound and driving down the floor for easy transition baskets. Derek knew he had to get back more quickly on defense. He succeeded in stealing the ball the next time, and the time after that he dogged his man so tightly that the kid threw up an air ball. Thanks to their defense, the Friars at least stayed close, at 16–11.

After a while the shots started to fall for Sam and Tyquan, but the Padres' shooters got hot as well. Derek headed for the bench with six minutes left in the half, and the Friars down, 22–18. Derek held his hand up to give Gio five, but Gio ignored him as he walked onto the court to replace him. Derek sat down, shaking his head. That kid was going to be a tough challenge.

But Gio sure could put on a show. As soon as play resumed, he took over the ball and didn't do much sharing. Except for the occasional lob to Marcus for the put-in at the basket, Gio completely hogged the ball. At least that was how Derek saw it.

Gio dribbled, drove, backed out when his way was blocked, and then either drove again or took the shot, no matter how well guarded he was. After a couple of minutes of this, the rest of the Friars found themselves standing around and watching Gio do his thing.

He didn't play much defense, either, other than going for steals while leaving his own man unguarded. Derek glanced at the coach a couple of times, wondering what he thought of Gio's performance on the court. It was impressive, for sure. He was a great ball handler and a good shooter, even when he didn't have clean looks at the basket.

It was hard to read Coach Nelson's face, though. He clapped and shouted when Gio hit a shot, and he barked at the team to pick things up on defense. But Derek couldn't tell what he thought of the way Gio was playing.

By the end of the half, the Friars were only three points behind at 31–28. Gio had scored the team's last eight points single-handedly. He high-fived everyone on the bench, except Derek, whom he gave a look that said, *There. That proves it. I deserve the starting job, and you don't.*

"All right, boys," Coach said as they gathered around in the locker room. "Not bad for our first time in combat. We're hanging in there. But we need to be getting open, not just standing around, okay? And let's pick up the effort on defense. We can't keep letting them take open jumpers."

The players were stealing glances at one another, wondering if the coach was talking about them. As for Derek, he was wondering if Coach would put him back in for the second half.

He didn't have to wait long to find out. "Gio, you stay in there," Coach told him. "Marcus, Sam, Tyquan, and Jose, you're in too. The rest of you, be ready."

Derek hung his head, disappointed. Obviously Coach Nelson had been impressed enough by Gio's dazzling display that he'd left him in there, and kept Derek on the bench.

For now, Derek told himself. *Don't take it personally.*

As long as Gio was red-hot, of course he would stay in the game. Coach Nelson was simply riding the hot hand. Derek knew he had to be prepared when his moment came again, as it surely would.

From the start of the second half, it was clear that Gio's shooting touch had gone cold. And instead of adjusting—passing the ball off or doing a pick-and-roll—Gio kept on trying to be a one-man show. He waved his teammates away from him, so he could have room to go one-on-one with his defender. Except he kept getting double-teamed, and either losing the ball or throwing up a brick.

The Padres, grabbing rebound after rebound, were running and gunning and racking up points. The Friar defense had all but collapsed in discouragement, unable to keep up with the Padres' speed in transition.

By the time the whistle blew for a St. Augustine time-out, there were ten minutes left in the game, with the Friars down by thirteen, 44–31, their biggest deficit so far.

Gio plunked himself down on the bench and threw a towel over his head, talking to no one. Marcus, too, had to sit down—his first break of the entire game. He was breathing hard and sweating bullets, clearly in need of a rest.

If the Friars, with Derek in the lead, didn't turn the tide right now, the Padres were going to run away with the game and put it out of reach. And Derek was going to have to do it without Marcus, the team's tallest player. The lineup he was leading was smaller than their opponents' at every single position.

"Okay, let's lock it down on defense," he told the other four on the floor with him: Sam at shooting guard; Jose at power forward; Costas Cypriotis, their second-string small forward; and Charlie Wong—in for Marcus at center—who was a full five inches shorter than the man he was guarding.

Derek started off with the ball, motioned to Charlie to

set a screen, and then drove left around him and powered his way to the basket. When the Padres' center went up to block the shot, Derek dished off to Jose, who banked in the layup, and got fouled to boot!

With the extra point on the free throw, the deficit was down to ten.

"Let's get some stops!" Derek yelled to his teammates. "Get back! Get back!"

They all hustled downcourt as fast as they could, forcing the Padres into a half-court set and slowing down their pace. Every Friar dogged his man, until the shot clock ran out and they got the ball back on the violation!

This time Derek passed off quickly, then ran to the corner, where he waited. Sam faked a jumper and quickly passed it to Derek, who drove to the base line and finally threw up a lob that Charlie jammed home!

With two minutes left they'd pulled within four, at 50–46, and now it was the Padres' coach calling a time-out!

Coach Nelson went over to Derek as he sat on the bench. Derek was tired, but not exhausted. He hoped the coach wasn't going to take him out for the homestretch.

"Derek, they're going to try to stop you from driving to the basket. You can pull up and take the jumper if you're open."

Derek nodded, feeling relieved to still be out there. But now it was time to bridge that final point gap. If they could get within a bucket, they could shake the Padres' confidence. They were already halfway there—Derek could feel it. But could he sink that key bucket when the time came?

Not if he thought too much about it, he realized as the whistle blew to resume play. Instead, Derek forced himself to concentrate on getting that first takeaway. Guarding the Padres' point guard, he reached in and knocked the inbounds pass away!

Sam was on it, and already driving to the basket. Derek trailed right behind him, and when the ball bounced off the rim, he went airborne to grab it and put it into the hoop!

The St. Augustine crowd was up and cheering now, making a deafening racket in the gym as the Friars got back on defense. Derek knew his mom and dad were out there, along with Sharlee, screaming their lungs out. He was determined to make them proud.

Watching the ball handler's eyes, and anticipating the no-look pass, Derek dived to his right and made the steal! From the ground he dished off to Sam, and this time Sam pulled up and made the game-tying jumper!

Less than a minute left now. The Padres were stymied by the suffocating defense the Friars were putting up. They finally launched one from way out. It missed, wide by a mile.

Derek got the rebound and brought the ball back down

the court. Then, seeing the Padre defenders fall away as they anticipated a drive to the basket, he pulled up, just like the coach had suggested, and took the open jumper— *SWISH!*

The Friars led by two!

"Woo-hoo!" Derek cried, raising his fist to the sky as he ran back downcourt.

The Padres were running out of time. They forced a quick shot that missed, but Jose committed a blocking foul, so the shooter went to the line. If he sank them both, the game would be tied again.

He hit the first shot—then missed the second! Derek grabbed the loose ball and ran down the court. About to be fouled on purpose, he let the long two-pointer fly—and hit it!

"No fouls! No fouls!" Coach yelled to them. The Padres were three points down, with not enough time to catch up. They missed one last shot—and the game was over!

The Friars all jumped up and down and hugged, thrilled to have notched their first victory. Afterward Derek went up to Gio, who'd ignored him during the celebration. "Good game," Derek told him.

"Yeah. You too." Gio reluctantly gave Derek a hand-shake, but there wasn't much enthusiasm behind it. And anyhow, his face gave away what he was really thinking:

It wouldn't have been so close if Coach had left me *in there.*

Chapter Eight

FOLLOW THE LEADER

"All right, men," said Coach Russell. "Take a look around at one another. These are the guys you'll be going into battle with for the next year, and maybe even beyond that. So, let's introduce ourselves one by one."

He nodded toward a slender kid Derek remembered trying out for second base. He'd stood out because he was six inches taller than any of the other prospects.

"My name is Mo," said the boy, who had something of an accent. "It's short for 'Mohammed,' actually. I'm originally from Somalia, in East Africa, but I live on the west side of Kalamazoo now. . . . Oh, and I'm an infielder."

"Thanks, Mo," said Coach Russell. "Next."

"Derek Jeter," said Derek. "I'm originally from New

Jersey, but I came to Kalamazoo when I was four. . . . Oh, and I'm an infielder as well."

"Next."

"Harry Hicks. I live over at Mount Royal Townhouses, same as Derek. We know each other and have played together before. And I'm going to be pitching."

"Hi, I'm Eli Warren," said another kid Derek remembered from tryouts. "Born and raised right down the block over there." He pointed toward right field. "So anytime I'm needed, I'm five minutes away." That got a laugh from the rest of the team.

"Okay. That's it for our new guys," said the coach. "Now for you veterans. Tell our first timers who you are."

Derek couldn't remember all their names right off the bat. But just looking at them, he knew he was among a group of really good athletes. He'd never been on a baseball team where you had to try out to make the squad, and he felt excited to be in such elite company.

The coaches started running instructional exercises out on the field, and for the next two hours, Derek forgot that the rest of the world existed. All three coaches were experts, and good teachers, too. Derek couldn't even imagine not being here! He was incredibly grateful to his parents for giving their go-ahead.

In between learning new things and having his strengths and weaknesses as a player surveyed by the coaches, Derek tried to get a sense of his teammates and their abilities. He already knew what Harry could do. Mo seemed to be built more for the outfield than second base—he was so tall, and really fast, too. But his skills at second made Derek wish Avery were his double-play partner instead.

Another thing Derek noticed was that the veterans on the team meshed as if they'd been playing together for a long time—which, of course, they had. They'd all been here the year before, except for Derek, Mo, Harry, and Eli.

Their three coaches worked a lot on situational awareness. You positioned yourself differently in the field depending on the game situation, the pitcher on the mound, the batter in the box, and the count.

Same for hitting. If your team was down a run, with two out in the last inning, it was time you went for broke. If there were two men on base because of walks, and nobody out, you might want to take a strike, try to hit it to the right side to advance the runners, or even bunt.

Derek already knew half the stuff he was learning, thanks to his dad, who'd been teaching him ever since Derek had been old enough to pick up a bat and glove.

But these coaches brought their own store of knowledge. Derek realized that if he was going to make it to the majors someday, he'd be needing input from lots of people along the way—not just his dad.

He could see how much he still had to learn, how much there was to know about the game. But he already loved being part of this team. It filled him with pride and self-confidence, and he couldn't wait to go for a championship with them next spring!

At basketball practice the next afternoon, Coach Nelson had his starters face off against the subs for a friendly scrimmage.

"We nearly lost that first game, and I know we're going to face better teams than the Padres," he said. "We've got St. Monica coming up pretty soon, and they're a perennial contender. We can't afford to play like we did last time."

The two sides went at it like their lives depended on it. Derek kept trying to collapse the other team's defense, then pass it to the open man.

On defense he was up against Gio, who kept trying to make Derek look bad by driving past him to the hoop. He succeeded once or twice just on sheer talent. But Derek was a dogged defender, and as the scrimmage went on, Gio had a harder and harder time getting off a shot, let alone making one.

One difference in the game was that Marcus, Gio's best bud, was on Derek's team. Marcus might have wished Gio were the starter, but once on the court he was all business. Every time Derek fed him with a lob or dished off to him under the rim, Marcus put the ball into the net.

Coach Nelson stopped them a few times, pointing out errors in defensive positioning and switch-offs, or poor spacing and weak screens on offense. He did encourage Gio to spread the ball around more. But that only made Gio more determined to show off what he could do on his own.

To be fair, he did sink a few spectacular shots, even with Derek draped all over him. The kid was a definite talent, Derek had to admit. But in Derek's opinion Gio wasn't yet ready to lead a team. Not by a long shot. And judging by the fact that Derek was still starting, Coach Nelson agreed.

After practice Derek went to shower before getting back into his street clothes and heading home on the late bus. As he entered the shower, he heard voices from two of the adjoining stalls.

Marcus and Gio.

". . . He's not that great," Marcus was saying. "Good passer, but you're a better shooter, for sure."

"I don't get why he's starting," Gio replied, an edge of anger in his voice. "I mean, basketball isn't even his number one sport!"

"Huh?"

"I'm telling you, the kid's crazy into *baseball*. I hear he plays *every day*, even in the winter!"

"Sheez!" Marcus said with a laugh. "That *is* crazy!"

"And get this—he's playing baseball *now*!"

"Now?"

"He's on the travel team!"

Derek kept quiet, wondering what they'd say about him next.

"If he cared about our team," Gio said, seething, "he'd quit travel ball right now and be all about basketball, like us." He shut off his water and stepped out of the stall.

Marcus followed suit. "Dang, man. I feel for you. I mean, dedication to the team should be rewarded."

"I know, right?"

They disappeared into the main locker room. Derek took his time showering, giving them a chance to get dressed and leave before he went back in there. He didn't want them knowing he'd heard every word they'd said!

Derek felt a wave of uneasiness shake his usual confidence. If Gio and Marcus knew he was playing two sports at once, it was only a matter of time before they complained about it to every other kid on the team. Would they follow Derek's lead then? Would they still trust in his commitment to the team?

Or would they believe the poisonous things Gio would say about him?

Chapter Nine

GUILT AND DREAD

"Class. Come to attention, please." Mr. Laithwaite's voice, quiet but commanding, drew instant silence. "I want to call to your attention that debates begin one week from today."

A murmur rippled through the room, then quickly died down again, as Mr. Laithwaite indicated that he wasn't finished. "Perhaps some of you have not been spending much time preparing. I know your workload so far has been more than you're used to . . ."

You can say that again, Derek thought. For the past two weeks he'd spent every spare moment reading textbooks and completing homework assignments. That is, every moment when he wasn't playing ball.

". . . but I suspect that many of you have not paid this assignment enough attention. My advice is to not put it off any longer. By now you should at least have marshaled your initial arguments and practiced delivering them— preferably in front of a mirror, or for your family members."

Derek had done no such thing. He'd jotted down a few talking points, about why sports were healthful and otherwise worthwhile, but he hadn't begun to shape them into a speech, let alone recite them out loud.

No way was he going to practice *anything* in front of his parents or Sharlee, that was for sure! Even the thought of doing it in front of a mirror, where he could see himself messing up in real time, made him uneasy.

"These debates will count heavily toward your first-semester grades," Mr. Laithwaite concluded, "so please take this unit as seriously as you would a midterm or final exam."

Derek only wished it *were* a midterm or final, instead of—no, he didn't even want to think about it!

And with Gary on the other side? That was just the sour cherry on top!

Derek glanced over at him. Gary was writing something down in a notebook, probably debating points to trip Derek up with.

He turned to look at Vijay, and noticed that his friend seemed really down. He was staring dully at his desk. Derek wondered what was going on with him. . . .

• • •

He soon found out. As they stood at their lockers after school, Vijay said, "So . . . you want to play some ball later on the Hill?"

Derek sighed. "Sorry, Vij, I can't."

"What is it this time? Practice again? Or another basketball game? I can't keep it all straight in my head."

Derek smiled. "Me neither. It's crazy, I know. But today I just have to stay in and work on the debate. You heard Mr. L."

"I know. But I'm already good to go."

"I'll bet you are," Derek said with a grin. "You're always totally prepared."

"You too," said Vijay. "Don't worry. You'll do fine."

"Ah, I don't think so. It's not exactly my thing. Plus, it's Gary, you know?"

"You'll be great," Vijay assured him. "You're defending sports, right? Who knows better about that than you? Surely not Gary!"

"Hmm . . ." Derek had to admit Vijay was right, as usual. So why did he still feel uneasy?

"So anyway . . . when do you think you'll have time again?"

Derek almost said, "Time for what?" But of course he already knew what Vijay meant. Time for friendship. Time for *Vijay*.

"Honestly, I don't know, Vij. By November first, for sure.

That's when travel ball is over. Till then we're just going to have to find time somehow. I don't know how."

"November? Kind of cold to be outside by then. . . ."

Derek sighed. "Well, I guess you and Avery, and whoever else, will have to get by without me till then."

"Not Avery."

"Huh?"

"They finally finished the renovations on her home field, so she and the guys haven't been around. It's just me, and sometimes Harry and Jeff. . . . A few others once in a while. . . ."

Poor Vijay. Derek felt awful for him. Losing Dave, Derek, and Avery, his three best friends, at the same time—he must have felt totally abandoned!

"Vij, we'll make up for lost time, I promise."

"I guess so. . . ."

"We'll have to hang out indoors, that's all."

"Sure thing. . . . Well. The bus is waiting. You coming?"

"In a minute. I've got to go down to the locker room and grab my uniform first. It needs a washing."

Derek took off down the hall, then down the stairs to the lower level, where the locker rooms were. The bus was waiting, and he didn't want it to leave without him, so he took the steps two at a time. But his mind was on Vijay all the while—until he missed a step and turned his ankle.

"OW!"

Derek winced, hopping around on the landing and

rubbing the sore spot. "Ow," he said again. "Owww."

It was really throbbing, but as he gingerly made his way to the locker room, the pain began to ease up slowly. *It's going to be okay,* he thought, relieved he hadn't hurt himself worse. *But, boy, that was dumb of me.*

He grabbed his dirty uniform, stuffed it into his book bag, and then headed back upstairs. He hoped the bus would still be waiting, but he was unable to speed up his pace.

He got there just in time and hobbled aboard.

"You okay?" Vijay asked as Derek sat down beside him.

"Yeah," Derek said, wincing again. "Missed a stair back there. Wasn't watching where I was going."

"Sounds bad."

"It's nothing," Derek assured Vijay, and himself, too. "I'll be fine. But I sure won't be taking the stairs two at a time anymore."

"For real," Vijay agreed with a laugh. "Haste makes waste."

"Ahem . . . ahem . . . *ahem*!"

Derek cleared his throat again and again. He looked at himself in the long mirror on the back of his closet door.

The kid staring back at him looked *terrified*. Derek tried to alter the image, but no matter what he did, the kid in the mirror didn't seem confident. Or prepared. Or ready.

He stared down at the sheet of paper with his main talking points and tried again:

"Sports are healthy. They're good for your body, good for your mind, and good for your spirit."

There. That sounded okay . . . almost.

The kid in the mirror had started to sweat. Derek wiped his brow, and his reflection did the same.

"Ahem! *Ahem!*"

Why was his throat so dry? Derek went into the bathroom and drew a cup of water from the sink. He gulped it right down, refilled the cup, and drank half before heading back into battle with himself.

"To continue . . ." He glanced down at his paper again. "Sports teach you how to interact with others, how to cooperate and get things done. You learn to follow the leader, and how to be a leader yourself."

Hmm. Did that sound weird?

No, he decided. It was the truth. In fact, it was exactly what he was doing these days—being a leader on the basketball squad, and following the leaders on the travel team, who were teaching him new tricks and enhancing his skills at every practice.

"Ahem . . ."

Derek poured the rest of the water in the cup down his parched throat. Back to the mirror again—and there was his reflection, still sweating.

This was agony! How was he going to get himself into debating shape in time for his big face-off with Gary?

Even if he managed that, he still had to get up in front

of *real kids*—not just his own awkward reflection! He could see them now . . . snickering, giggling, and enjoying his utter humiliation.

Time for a break? Derek looked at his alarm clock. It was already 7:30. No, he'd better push on.

"Sports helped integrate the country, before the country was integrated."

That was a good line. He could talk about Jackie Robinson and all.

"And participation brings great possibilities for boys and girls."

Also good. He could talk about Avery and tell her story. With a few stories like that, he could fill up his entire five minutes!

Derek looked at the clock again: 7:45. Was it too late to call Vijay and get some help?

No, Derek decided. If the shoe were on the other foot, he would want Vijay to call him.

He dialed quickly.

"Hello?"

"Hi, it's me," Derek said.

"Hey! What's up?"

"I'm in trouble. Can you help me practice my debating stuff?"

"Sure! When?"

"Tomorrow after school? No, wait. I have a game tomorrow afternoon. . . . How about the day after? Oh, wait. I've got travel team practice. . . . Can you do it tomorrow? Like, at seven?"

"My place or yours?"

"Yours. I'll confirm with my parents to make sure that's okay," Derek said. Otherwise Sharlee would want to watch, and Derek wasn't ready for an audience yet.

"You got it," Vijay said, yawning. "Hey, what time is it?"

"Time for you to go to bed. Sorry about calling so late, but it's an emergency."

"I guess so!"

"You can practice yours in front of me, too," Derek offered, as if Vijay needed the help. Talking in front of a classroom of people was no problem at all for him, lucky guy.

Derek hung up and tried to get back to work, but it was no use. His brain was fried, and he was starting to get cold chills just thinking about his upcoming date with destiny.

If the kids wound up laughing at him, he'd just shrivel up and die!

He sat on the side of the bed, his head in his hands, beads of sweat trickling down his forehead and his back. *Nervous* sweat. Not the healthy kind.

There was a soft knocking at the door. "Derek?" His father's voice. "Can I come in?"

"Uh-huh." Derek sat up, but there was no disguising the state he was in.

"You sick?"

"In a way. I'm trying to practice for the debate, but . . ."

"Oh. I get you." His dad sat down next to him on the bed and patted Derek's knee. "You know, I used to be terrified of getting up in front of people and giving a speech."

"You were?"

"Oh yeah. My legs would just start shaking and shaking. . . ."

Derek smiled, picturing it. "Seriously? What did you do, Dad?"

"Lucky for me, I had a teacher who noticed how nervous I was, and recommended that I try standing behind a podium at the front of the room. I just stood behind it, so no one could see my legs." His dad chuckled. "It worked, too. I got an A! And I eventually did get used to talking in front of folks. The more you do it, you know?"

"Hopefully never again after this!"

"Don't say that, Derek. Listen, you want to play in the major leagues someday, right?"

"Yeah . . ."

"Well, you're going to have to do interviews with the press, give speeches at charity events, stuff like that. It's better to get over your fears now, when there's not that much at stake."

"*Not that much?* Are you kidding? They're all going to be laughing at me!"

"Why would they do that? Is there something funny about you? No. Is there something funny about what you're saying? I assume not."

"And if I'm sweating all over, and my legs and hands are shaking, and I'm stumbling over my words?" Derek could hear his voice rising, so he lowered it to a near-whisper. "I don't even care who wins, Dad. I just want it to be over with."

His dad sighed, shaking his head. "Derek, you're not the only one who's scared of what people might think of them. I just told you my story. Most people are scared at least some of the time, about one thing or another. It's the price of being human."

Derek let the thought sink in.

"Remember, old man. Courage isn't about not being afraid. It's about doing what you're afraid of, because *it has to be done*."

Chapter Ten

BY THE SKIN OF THEIR TEETH

"We're going with the same starting lineup as last game," Coach Nelson told the team. "Everybody ready?"

The Friars all shouted, "YEAH!"

But Derek could see that Gio's heart wasn't in it. He slammed his locker door shut and headed into the gym on his own, instead of with the rest of the team.

Derek's ankle was still throbbing a little from when he twisted it the day before on the stairs, but not enough for him to say anything to Coach Nelson. Derek wasn't about to give up his starting role to Gio—not when he was being counted on to be a team leader!

Today the Friars were at home for the second straight game, facing the Wolves of Williams Academy. Derek didn't recognize any of their players, and he had no idea how good they were. On the other hand, that meant the Wolves had no idea what the Friars could do either.

Gio was sitting at the far end of the bench with a towel over his head, even though he hadn't broken a sweat yet. The rest of the team gathered around Coach Nelson.

Derek wondered if the coach noticed Gio sitting apart. If he did, he didn't let on. "Let's go get 'em!" he said, and the team let out a yell and high-fived one another as the starters headed onto the court for the opening tip.

Marcus outjumped the other center, and Derek grabbed the loose ball. He drove down the court and, seeing that he had a lane to the basket, took it to the hoop for an easy layup!

He hustled back on defense. The Wolves' small forward threw up a wild shot, and when Marcus grabbed the rebound, Derek was already flying back down the court, a step ahead of his man. Marcus hit him on the fly. Derek stopped, pulled up, and hit the open jumper!

Four minutes later the Friars had a 10–3 lead. Eight of those points were Derek's, but he knew that one of his biggest jobs was to spread the ball around. The next time downcourt he drove the lane, looking to dish off to the open man.

But no one was open—and Derek, sinking a beautiful floater, was simply taking what the defense was giving him.

Running back on defense after scoring his tenth point, he stole a glimpse at Gio. He was following Derek's every move, with eyes that looked like hot coals.

Wait till I get my chance, Derek could almost hear him thinking. *I'll show everyone who's got the better game!*

For his part Derek was starting to feel the effects of all that early effort. His ankle was throbbing now, worse than before. Still, he thought he could play through it.

Ten minutes in, Coach Nelson made a bunch of substitutions, putting Gio in along with the rest of the second team. Derek tried not to limp as he walked back to the bench.

He didn't look at Gio as they passed. Derek was handing him a ten-point lead. If Gio could build on it, or at least hold the fort, so much the better for the whole team.

"You okay, Jeter?" Coach Nelson asked him as play resumed.

"Huh?"

"Your leg. Something wrong?"

"No, no, I'm fine, Coach. Good to go."

Coach Nelson nodded. Having heard what he wanted to hear, he turned his attention back to the game. Derek rubbed his sore ankle when the coach wasn't looking.

Gio was out there being Gio, slicing and dicing his way through the Wolves' defense, forcing impossible shots instead of passing the ball to his teammates.

And yet most of those impossible shots were going in!

Gio's moves even got whoops and hollers from the home crowd, a few of them holding up signs that said G.O. GIO! and WE LOVE GIO!!

If Gio's "showtime" style got the fans going, that was fine with Derek. He wasn't after attention and fan worship. He just wanted his team to win, and if Gio was getting it done, who cared if he was the fans' favorite?

Gio finished out the half with a flourish that left the Friars up 40–24, and they all headed back to the locker room to chants from the crowd of "G.O.! G.O.! G.O.!" For once Gio seemed happy. It was good to see the kid smile, even if his triumph was kind of at Derek's expense.

During the halftime break Derek avoided rubbing his ankle, lest anyone notice. But he had to admit it was really bothering him. He was almost relieved when Coach Nelson left Gio in to start the second half.

Derek wondered if Coach Nelson had made the switch because of his ankle, or because of Gio's play on the court. As the minutes passed, he could feel the throbbing ease. He massaged it whenever Coach was busy watching the game.

Gio was still taking too many shots, but Derek didn't really blame him, because the Wolves weren't swarming the man with the ball. In fact, they were practically goading Gio to shoot. It hadn't worked for them in the first half. But now Derek saw that the Wolves' strategy might have a logic behind it. Because Gio's shooting touch soon went stone-cold. He was still taking all the shots, but he wasn't making *any* of them—not that it kept him from trying again the next time down the court.

Before Derek knew it, the Friars' lead had been cut to only six. Coach Nelson called time and told Derek he was going in.

Derek was determined this time to concentrate on defense. On offense he would slow things down and look to dish off to his teammates—especially Sam and Marcus. They'd been standing around on the court, not really participating in the offense. They'd lost focus and turned the ball over, and they'd lost some of their usual hustle, too.

Derek was determined to get them back on their toes, and the only way to do that was to get them the ball!

For the rest of the game, he forgot about his ankle—except for every time he jumped and landed on it. Then he'd wince, take one limping step, and get right back into the action.

Most of the time he was fine, and playing tenacious defense. A good thing, too. Because although he was feeding his teammates the ball, they hadn't shot much all game, and it took a while for them to find the range.

The game stayed close until the final minute—when Derek made a key steal, drew a foul, and hit both shots to cement the victory!

The Friars all high-fived, and the crowd left happy and raucous. But the mood was not so great once they got back to the locker room.

Coach Nelson was most upset of all. "I've gotta say," he began, shaking his head, "that was a scary experience. If you guys can't hold a big lead against a team like the Wolves, how are we gonna beat St. Monica next game, the division winners from last year? You guys play the way you did today, and we're gonna get creamed! What happened to all the stuff we practiced? Where was the teamwork? Where was the focus?"

The Friars sat, dead silent. There was no good answer to his question.

"Let me lay it out for you," he went on. "I don't want to see this kind of play again. We've got to start sharing the ball. When half the team isn't getting any touches, they lose focus, and they make mistakes. They commit stupid fouls, they turn the ball over, they lose the easy rebound because they get outhustled."

He looked around the room. "I want every one of you to ask yourselves, 'What could I have done better?' This team has too much talent to play like we did today."

He blew out a long breath. "All right. That's it for now. See you all Monday at three. Be on time—the bus leaves at three ten—and *be better*."

Chapter Eleven

DIFFICULT DAYS

"Good for developing bodies and minds . . . right . . ." Vijay was looking over Derek's debating points, nodding as he read.

Derek sat next to his friend on the sofa in the Patels' living room, massaging his sore left ankle. He didn't want it bugging him tomorrow during baseball practice. Better to stop any swelling right away.

"You know," said Vijay, "you could also add something about group cooperation. Like, how sports help you figure out how to take on different roles, in order to achieve group success?"

"That's brilliant," Derek said, taking the index cards back from Vijay and jotting down his new argument.

"Okay, now try it again, from the beginning—looking at *me* this time, instead of the floor."

"Aw, come on, Vij. Do I have to?"

"Derek, this is like a trial in a courtroom. You're the lawyer. If you're going to win the case, you have to connect with the jury."

"But it makes me too nervous looking people in the eye like that! What if they look away, or make a face at me? What if they crack up laughing at me?"

"Just look at each person for one or two seconds, then shift to the next for a couple of seconds, et cetera. Not long enough to worry about what they're thinking. You saw how I did mine before, right?"

Vijay had started off their work session by going first, rattling off his arguments against raising the driving age to nineteen. He'd looked Derek straight in the eye every now and then, and Derek had to admit that it was very effective.

But when it was his turn, Derek kept getting a lump stuck in his voice box. He wound up clearing his throat over and over again, fighting dry mouth, wet armpits, shaking legs, and goose bumps on his arms.

Awful.

He forced himself to go through his presentation one more time. This time he tried to look up from his index cards as often as he could, glancing at Vijay, who nodded encouragingly in return.

But halfway through, Derek lost his place, and he had to waste ten seconds getting back into his argument. Not a good thing when you only have five minutes to make your points.

"Concentrate on what you're trying to tell me, Derek. Don't worry about what I'm thinking. You're offering me precious jewels of knowledge! Important things I need to know about sports! Tell me. Go ahead."

Derek continued, this time really concentrating on what he was saying about the subject. It helped. He finished without any further problems.

"That's it!" Vijay said. "I think you've got the idea now."

"Well, I guess it's time to wrap this up," Derek said. "Thanks a bunch, Vij. At least now I feel like I've got a fighting chance."

"When a person is as competitive as you are, Derek, a fighting chance is all he needs."

By the next morning Derek's ankle was feeling pretty good. Not that he didn't get that tiny twinge now and then, reminding him that it still wasn't 100 percent.

As his dad drove him and Harry over to practice, Derek was thinking he'd go easy on his body today. The big basketball game was coming up, after all, and he wanted to be in tip-top shape so he could lead the Friars against St. Monica.

He figured he would just tell Coach Russell what was up with his leg, and the coach would understand and take it easy on him today. But before Derek could get a moment with him, the coach gathered the entire team around him.

"All right, men. Instead of our regular practice next Saturday, I've arranged a game with the East Side Eagles, at their field."

That brought an excited cheer from the players. But the coach wasn't done talking.

"So, I've been watching you all go through your paces, and I may want to make some changes. For today's practice I want to play around with positions a bit. Just as a kind of experiment—for fun, okay? No need for anybody to get nervous or upset."

The players all looked at one another. Some seemed fine with the coach's plan. Others looked worried.

Derek was positively *alarmed*. He'd *already* won the shortstop job—or so he'd thought! He'd certainly played there the bulk of the time at practice. . . .

Harry, seated next to him, leaned over and whispered, "Nate wants to play short, and Eli wants to be a starter. I heard Coach tell their dads he'd give them another look."

Derek was stunned. Apparently, nothing was set in stone after all!

In fact, when Coach sent them out into the field, Derek was put at third base. Nate Wallace, last year's third baseman, was standing in Derek's usual spot. Mo was on the mound, with Eli at second, while Harry stood in the box with a bat in his hands.

Derek pounded his fist into his mitt. He'd relaxed his guard after making the team, and now he regretted it. He was going to have to prove all over again that he belonged at shortstop—*but how?*

Nate was a good athlete, taller and huskier than Derek. He hit for more power, too—so third base would have been the natural spot for him. But Nate wanted to play shortstop, and he'd been on the travel team for two years, so he and the coach had a long history together.

Derek saw the big picture now. It wasn't just this practice. For the rest of the fall season, Coach Russell was going to play around with positions and batting orders, trying to solidify roles for the spring, when it would really count.

Derek had to wonder, If he did well at third base, would that hurt his cause or help it? Unfortunately, he knew he could never give any less than his best.

Besides, if he *didn't* play well, Eli was waiting in the wings to be given a regular spot! No way did Derek want to wind up as the alternate, playing a different position every game, or if everyone showed up, not playing at all!

He fielded a grounder, and his ankle chose that moment to remind him that it was still not completely healed.

But there was no question of telling the coach about it now. He was just going to have to grit his teeth and prove he belonged at shortstop!

He managed to make a decent showing at third. And

when Coach had him pitch an inning, Derek surprised himself with the speed on his fastball. Where had that come from? He hadn't been able to throw that hard last season, the few times he'd had to pitch!

But later, legging out a pair of hits, Derek found himself altering his stride so that his left ankle wouldn't take too much of a pounding. He didn't want it flaring up again, no matter what!

Derek was unusually quiet on the ride home. He hadn't gotten to play short the whole day! Nate had spent the whole practice there instead, leaving Derek wondering if he'd just lost his prized position for good.

At least he hadn't reinjured his ankle. It actually felt okay, considering what he'd just put it through. But now his right *calf* felt distinctly weird and crampy. Derek knew it was from the change in his gait to protect the ankle. He sure hoped it would calm down in time for the big game on Monday. Because if he'd had to go out there right now, he wasn't sure he could do it!

More icing tonight, for sure, he thought.

But he couldn't keep the image of Kurt Carsten out of his mind, *or* get his dad's words out of his ears:

"You've got to work smart, not just hard. Carsten should have sat himself down if he wasn't right."

Chapter Twelve

THE BREAKING POINT

After school on Monday, Derek got off the team bus and walked into the St. Monica visitors' locker room without the slightest hint of a limp, ready to lead his team into battle, no matter how many dirty looks Gio shot him.

On the way there Coach Nelson had named Derek the starter for today's game. Gio's jaw had dropped in disbelief, and he'd seemed like he was about to protest, but there was no way he could have sounded off without everyone seeing and hearing, so he'd kept his frustration to himself—*barely*.

He'll get his chance again one day, Derek reflected.

Gio was really good, with skills as good as Derek's or better. But he wasn't playing in his driveway or on the playground anymore. This was big-time middle school basketball! There were five guys on each team, not two or three. Gio still needed to learn to play team ball, and today Derek meant to show him how it was done.

Once the game started, Derek put all thoughts of Gio out of his head. Each time he ran down the court, he tested out his ankle and calf, and was pleased to note that they didn't hurt at all.

The Friars shot out to an early lead, 16–5, thanks to hot shooting by Sam and Tyquan. Derek kept the team running down the floor at a fast pace, putting the St. Monica Angels on their heels. He kept harassing his man on defense, until the kid got frustrated, shoved Derek, and was called for a charging foul!

After a few minutes of running full speed, backing up in a hurry, and shifting from side to side to cover his man, Derek's calf began to feel tired and achy again. There weren't many fouls being called, so no pauses in the action for him to rest.

None of the players were getting a chance to breathe, so Coach Nelson called a time-out just five minutes into the game, and sat the Friars' starting five down.

Gio practically ran out onto the court, clapping his hands and hopping up and down. Derek sat on the bench to watch the show. "Go, Gio!" he shouted, cupping his hands in front of his mouth.

Gio ignored him. He took the ball, ran it downcourt,

and tossed a no-look lob right into a leaping Charlie's hands for the easy put-in! *A beautiful assist,* Derek noted, impressed. Had Gio been listening to Coach Nelson's words after all?

Gio did dish the ball off once or twice more. But he spent a lot of time playing his usual one-on-one isolation game. The only time he passed was when he got double-teamed.

When the Angels called time-out with seven minutes left in the half, the Friars were still up by eight points, just three less than when Derek had first sat down.

Now Coach put him in there, and Derek quickly got the team back to playing as a unit. The Friar defense firmed up right away, resulting in two quick takeaways that turned into easy buckets. Derek could tell the whole team was feeling it, and they were building up momentum, too.

Then suddenly, while he was diving for a loose ball, Derek's calf cramped up. He grabbed the ball as two St. Moni᠎ n players tried to yank it away, and held on until the refs called jump ball.

Trying to stand up, Derek found he couldn't put his full weight on his leg without his calf going into full cramp mode.

When Coach saw the state he was in, he called time-out. Derek limped back to the bench, his leg grabbing at him. "Ow!" he said, wincing as he sat down. "Owwww . . ."

Gio was already back out there, and the whistle blew for play to resume.

"You okay, Jeter?" the coach asked, looking worried.

"It's just a cramp, Coach."

"Okay, well, just sit the rest of the half, and let's see where we are." The coach turned his attention back to the game. The look of worry on his face didn't go away, though. In fact, it got worse—especially after the Friars lead started to shrink.

By the end of the half, they were up by only six, at 39–33. They'd scored all of five points since Derek had limped to the bench, while the Angels had tallied fourteen. Only Gio's scoring had kept St. Augustine from falling behind altogether.

Back in the locker room Coach came over to where Derek was sitting. "How's it doing?"

Derek could feel the cramp easing up. "Better. I think I can go."

Coach Nelson nodded, frowning. "Well, let's let Gio start the half. Give it a few more minutes to calm down, huh?" He patted Derek on the back and went over to give Gio the news.

The second half began pretty much the way the first had ended. The Friars were being outplayed, and Gio was still dominating the offense to the exclusion of his frustrated teammates. Marcus kept yelling for the ball with no success, even though he was wide open under the basket.

Derek went on massaging his calf. Finally, just when the Friars fell behind for the first time, he told the coach he was ready to go back in.

"Time-out!" Coach Nelson yelled, beckoning his team off the court. "Okay, Derek, you're back in there. You sure you're okay now?"

Derek nodded. He really did feel all right, though not perfect by any means.

"Okay, let's go!" The coach clapped his hands, and Derek jogged back onto the court with the rest of the starting five.

At first he was able to get up and down the court with the other players, and the Friars narrowed the gap to 49–45. After a couple of minutes Derek completely forgot he was nursing an injury.

Then, with the score 51–48, Angels, he went up for a rebound and landed hard on his ankle. Shooting pains ran up his calf, and he dropped to the floor, grabbing his leg as the cramp came back big-time.

Coach Nelson called time-out again. Marcus and Sam helped Derek get to the bench, because right then he couldn't do it on his own. He knew he'd aggravated both his ankle and his calf.

Now he wished he'd taken himself out back in the first half!

Derek watched the rest of the big game from the bench, as St. Monica pulled away from the Friars. The Angels used every second of time they could, killing the clock and denying St. Augustine a chance to come back.

Gio played a little less selfishly—but the team still lost,

and that was what mattered most to Derek. He felt in his heart that the Friars could have won the game if only he'd been in there leading the charge. But when crunch time had come, he'd been on the bench. *Useless!*

He'd messed everything up. How had he let it get to this point? Why had he played at baseball practice on Saturday? If he'd sat out then, he wouldn't have hurt his calf trying to protect his ankle!

Now he was in real trouble. It was going to take several days, if not weeks, for him to heal. And where did that leave him for the baseball game this coming Saturday?

Exactly nowhere.

"What do you mean, it's been hurting you for a while?"

Mr. Jeter sat in the big chair, opposite the couch where Derek lay on his back, with his left leg elevated on the armrest. His mother looked on from the other armchair. Sharlee had just gone up to bed, which was why they hadn't talked about it till now.

"I don't understand," said Mrs. Jeter. "You say it's been bothering you for almost a week. Didn't you ever think to rest it? Didn't you think *to tell us*?"

Derek was more disappointed in himself than angry. "I know, Mom. I should've paid more attention, and I should have told you before. But it *wasn't that bad*. I thought I could play through it."

"That's what Carsten said too. Now he's out for the rest

of the season." Mr. Jeter picked up the remote and shut off the ball game. "We talked about this, Derek. I really thought you were paying attention."

"Sorry, Dad. I know it was dumb of me. But Coach Russell was reshuffling our positions, and I didn't want to beg off practice. I thought he might demote me to alternate or something!"

"Derek," his mom broke in. "Your coach would have understood. Injuries happen. If you say you're okay to play, they have to trust you're telling them the truth."

"I'm sorry, Mom," Derek said again. It was fast becoming his new mantra. But really, what else was there for him to say? He'd messed up royally.

If he'd rested his ankle when he'd first hurt it, he would probably have healed by now. And yes, he'd seen the great Kurt Carsten just make the same mistake. Derek knew he should have paid more attention, and learned.

But he hadn't, and now it was too late. Everything he'd wanted to do—leading the basketball team to the playoffs, impressing Coach Russell with his play at shortstop—he'd put it *all* at risk!

"You know, Derek," his dad said, "when we gave you permission to play both sports, it was on the condition that you still take care of yourself. I would say this violates that promise. Wouldn't you, Dot?"

His mom nodded sadly, and sighed. "From here on in, Derek, you're going to have to pull back some. You'll have to make time for your body to rest, just like you make time for your schoolwork—even if it means you miss practices here and there."

"But the coaches—"

"They'll have to understand," Mr. Jeter said with finality.

"Trust them, Derek," his mom urged. "I'm sure this isn't the first time they've had to deal with this kind of problem."

Derek nodded. He was relieved that they weren't saying he had to quit one of his teams altogether!

"For now," his dad said, "no playing anything until you get clearance from the doctor."

"But—"

His dad already knew what he'd been going to say. "And you heard the doctor. You can forget about any sports for at least a week, no matter how good your leg feels. Clear?"

"Yes, Dad."

"All right, then. Dot?"

"I'm good. Derek, you want some ointment on it before bed?"

"Thanks, Mom."

She went to get it. Derek sat up and started massaging his calf. "It's already better . . . a little."

"Mmm." His dad seemed unimpressed. He looked at his watch. "It's eight thirty. You'd better call Coach Russell and give him the bad news. I'll go get the cordless phone."

Derek felt sick to his stomach as he delivered the bad news. He could hear the disappointment in the coach's voice.

"I'm surprised, Derek. I knew your leg was an issue, because you kept rubbing it at practice. But that was days ago. I surely thought it'd be healed by now."

Derek had to tell him all about the basketball game, and how he'd aggravated the injury by staying on the court when he should have rested it. Then he had to listen to the coach tell him exactly what his parents had just told him—that he should have been up-front about any health issues.

"I know, Coach. I'm really, really sorry. It won't happen again, I promise. *Never.*"

"All right, Derek. Keep me posted, and let us know when you're ready to come back, okay?"

"Sure thing, Coach."

"Good night. Let's hope you heal up soon."

"Yeah." Derek blew out a breath as he hung up.

What did he have to look forward to now? No baseball game Saturday, no basketball game next week. . . .

Oh, wow. The next thing he had to look forward to was *his debate with Gary*!

Chapter Thirteen

SITTING IT OUT

On Saturday morning, as the West Side travel team played its first game of the fall season, Derek sat on the bench, watching. He felt an ache in his heart as he watched Nate playing shortstop.

He was playing really well, too. In the first two innings he made three sparkling plays on hard-hit balls, keeping the East Siders off the bases and off the scoreboard.

It was *agony* not being out there! Still, Derek cheered Nate on. To him the team always came first, no matter what. His dad had drummed that into his head since Derek was three or four, and it had sunk in deeply.

"Way to go, Nate!" he yelled, clapping and whooping—trying somehow to be part of it, to let his teammates know he was there for them, even if he couldn't get onto the field. Harry came over a couple of times to give him a pat on the back, which was nice of him, and did make Derek feel a little better for a minute or two.

But the pain of being left out soon returned. And it got worse in the third inning, when Harry gave up four runs on three hits and two walks.

Coach Russell shifted him over to third and let Mo have a turn at pitching. It didn't go well on either end. Mo couldn't get the ball over. He walked two more runs in before *finally* inducing a pop-up to third—where Harry dropped the ball, extending the inning even further!

Although they did manage to put some late runs across, the West Siders lost in the end, 8–5. A six-run hole had proved too deep for them to dig out of.

To Derek, watching from the bench, the game seemed to take forever. He gathered with his downcast teammates afterward, trying to pick up their spirits, though his own were on the ground.

"Thanks, man," said Nate. "Thanks for showing up today. Class act."

They tapped gloves, and for the first time all day, Derek felt a little better. He saw that it was different here than in Little League. Every kid on this team lived and breathed baseball, and dreamed of playing in the big leagues just like he did.

The very fact that he was here, wearing the same

uniform, meant that he belonged. Derek felt like he'd graduated to a different level somehow, where everyone took the game more seriously.

To Nate he was already a teammate, no matter where Coach put them on the field or in the batting order. Who-ever wound up being the alternate would be an equal among equals too—and that suited Derek just fine. If it wound up being him, he'd be devastated, but he wouldn't quit, or give up his long-term ambitions.

He was silent and thoughtful on the way home. On the one hand, Coach Russell had thanked him for showing up and rooting hard for the team. That was good. On the other hand, they'd lost their first game as a team, big-time. And unfortunately for Derek, Nate had played well at short, while going 2 for 4 at the plate.

Even so, Derek couldn't help feeling what he'd felt at the basketball game—that if only he'd been healthy and playing, at whatever position, the team might have won. It wasn't a logical feeling, but there it was. And Derek didn't know how to shake it.

Then came the Friars' big game against Poly Prep. It was one thing for Derek to sit and watch a kid like Nate, whom he liked and respected, take over his position at shortstop. It was another to watch Gio starting in his place.

Gio was supremely talented, but he was no kind of team leader—nor even a good teammate a lot of the time. The

Friars still had a winning record, but they weren't playing even close to their best.

Derek had a bad feeling about this game. The Poly Prep Tornadoes, winners of the Kalamazoo northern division, had beaten St. Monica, the southern division winners, in the playoffs to become last year's district champions. They'd even come in fourth statewide! Not only that, but they had four of their five starters back from last year. St. Augustine had only two—Jose and Tyquan.

If Gio was going to play the same ball-hogging, hot-dogging game of hoops he usually did, the Friars didn't have a chance.

Derek had traveled across town with the team. He knew that his showing up meant a lot to them. As the other players got changed in the visitors' locker room, Derek found himself giving one-on-one pep talks, reminding them that no matter what, they had to give maximum energy and play tight, active defense.

Derek noticed that the coach was having a stern private talk with Gio, who kept nodding, and glancing over at Derek every now and then.

Derek thought he knew why. It wasn't the first time he'd seen Coach Nelson take Gio aside like this. But so far it hadn't yielded results—or at least, none that lasted very long. Derek sure hoped this time would be different, for the team's sake.

• • •

From the first tip-off, Derek found himself leaning forward in his seat, so totally into the game that it was like he was on the court.

He tried to *will* himself into Gio's brain: *Drive the left lane! Pass off to Sam. He's wide open in the corner! Get back on D! Get back!* And so on.

Remarkably, Gio seemed to be listening! On the team's first possession, he found Marcus under the basket for a flashy layup. Next time, he dished off to Sam for another easy bucket. He grabbed a takeaway on defense, then lobbed one up for Marcus, who finger-rolled it home!

Five minutes into the game Gio finally took his first shot—and only because Poly Prep was leaving him wide open after so many assists. Of course the shot went in. Derek was so excited, he forgot to be miserable about not playing. Gio was finally showing signs of *getting* it!

For weeks Derek had been trying to show the way with his own play at point guard. And Coach had been on Gio's case too, with no effect—till now. Maybe it was the fact that Derek was out of the picture. With him sidelined Gio didn't have to think as much about impressing the coach. He didn't have to try to grab the starting slot—Derek had gone and handed it to him.

Derek had a swirl of mixed feelings. But overall he was pretty pumped. If Gio was going to play like this, the Friars would soon be playoff-bound—*and dangerous*!

Derek was amazed at how well the team was responding.

With Gio getting them all into the mix, they were alert and on the balls of their feet, hustling and muscling and grabbing every loose ball and rebound! Even their shooting looked better.

Poly Prep, the reigning district champions, were looking panicked and overmatched. They were all expert sharpshooters, though, so they still scored a lot of points. Still, by halftime the Friars lead was 45–30, a fifteen-point margin!

It had been an offensive explosion, and even Derek was blown away. Marcus alone had scored twelve points in the first half, showing what he was capable of when he got the ball in his hands near the basket. Sam had drained four buckets and a couple of free throws for ten points of his own.

And Gio had gone the entire first half without sitting down once, and his play hadn't suffered, even as the clock had wound down.

The mood in the locker room was jubilant. "Let's keep it up for the second half!" Coach Nelson said, clapping his hands. "You guys are looking great out there!"

For a second Derek felt left out. He wondered if Coach would begin reconsidering who got the start going forward. But now was not the time to worry about that, he knew. Not when the Friars were about to beat the reigning district champs!

The second half started the same way the first had

ended. Seven minutes in, the Friars lead had ballooned to twenty points.

And then, for some strange reason, a switch must have flipped in Gio's brain. Because all of a sudden he went back to showboating—taking unnecessarily difficult shots instead of looking to set up his open teammates.

The Poly Prep players were not happy about getting shown up, either—and they let Gio know in no uncertain terms. The refs rushed in to separate the players before anything got out of hand.

It was an ugly scene. Coach Nelson was furious, barking at his team, and sending the hottest-tempered players back to the bench to cool off—including Gio, who was thrown out of the game along with the kid guarding him. He moved Sam Rockman to point guard, where he'd never played before. Sam was a shooter, not a strong ball-handler or passer.

Poly Prep made a last-ditch charge, narrowing the gap to twelve. But with time running out, St. Augustine's second-stringers were able to hold them off and seal the victory—final score, 65–51.

The Friars were happy to get the big win, of course. But as they packed up their gear for the bus ride home, Derek could sense that some of the shine had come off their victory.

Coach Nelson spent most of the trip giving them a stern lecture about sportsmanship. "What makes me angriest," he told them, "is that *our* team had a hand in starting the trouble."

Gio looked straight ahead of him, still steaming—not that he said a word to Coach Nelson. He wouldn't have dared. But his face always gave him away. Derek could read his thoughts, loud and clear: Gio was convinced he hadn't done anything wrong. Never mind that he'd been practically taunting the other team, dribbling the ball between defenders' legs and stuff, when the Friars had already had a big lead and the game had been almost over.

In Gio's mind the Tornadoes had started the pushing and shoving for no good reason. There was no regret in Gio's burning gaze, even though he'd wound up getting ejected.

As Derek got off the bus at his corner, he thought about all he'd missed this past week. He'd learned his lesson, all right—and it had been painful in every way.

But he knew it would never happen to him again, because *he wouldn't let it*. In future if he wasn't in playing shape, he'd say something right away—even if it wound up costing him playing time and displeasing the coach.

But had *Gio* learned *his* lesson? He'd figured out how to share the ball, finally, so maybe there was hope. But Gio was as stubborn as he was talented. Derek knew he had to keep trying to get through to him and hope Gio would get the message one day.

Derek wondered how long it would be before he was ready to play. His leg was feeling a lot better than it had the week before. Maybe he could convince the doctor to let him play in a few days. . . .

But when the time came, would he be given either of his old jobs back? What if he had to ride the bench on both teams?

Just thinking about it, he started to feel sick to his stomach, and he was glad when he stepped inside and smelled dinner in the oven. Queasiness gave way to hunger, and he put away his worries, at least for the moment.

Just heal up, he told himself. *Then let the chips fall where they may.*

Chapter Fourteen

ULTIMATE COMBAT

In late September pairs of kids had started their debates. Each time two names were called, Derek cringed, hoping his and Gary's turn hadn't come yet. Days went by, and still their names weren't called.

In a way it might have been better if they'd been the first ones chosen. That way, at least, Derek could have gotten it over with and recovered from the ordeal by watching the other kids debate.

But no such luck. Every day, two pairs had their debates, and the winners were chosen by the rest of the class. On the fourth day, Vijay went up against Marcus and won handily. Derek was glad for him, but Vijay didn't seem too excited by his victory. Those kinds of things came easily to him. And something told Derek his old friend was missing him.

Derek missed Vijay, too—even more so now that he had to sit there and *watch* his teams play without him.

At least the Friars had kept on winning. Gio was now firmly ensconced as the starting point guard. Although he was still taking about half the team's shots, Coach had stopped riding him so hard about it. Derek figured it was because the team was winning against a couple of weaker opponents on the schedule. Still, Coach Nelson kept asking Derek how his leg was feeling.

"Better," Derek would answer, "but not *all* better yet."

For the last ten days it had felt like he was living in slo-mo. Practices dragged on forever. Derek still managed to pick up some pointers from the coaches, but it was all in his head, since he couldn't practice any of it.

He did feel a little better with each passing day. But every time he thought about telling his coaches he was ready to play again, he thought about Kurt Carsten and what had happened to him when he'd come back too early.

Derek didn't want to spoil the rest of the season *in two sports* just because he was too impatient to let himself heal. That would make a bad situation even worse!

And of course a *doctor* was going to have to agree.

In the second week of October, on the very last day of debates, Derek finally heard his and Gary's names called. Even though he'd known it was coming, when it actually happened, it felt like a total shock.

Derek reached into his book bag and pulled out his note cards. On his way to the front of the room, he promptly dropped them, and had to pick them all up from under the feet of his laughing classmates.

Great. Great start, Derek, he told himself. He could hear the drumbeat of his own heart, thundering in his ears as he faced the jury of his classmates, and the dreaded judge, Mr. Laithwaite, who now announced, "Resolved: schools should cut back on sports teams and activities, and concentrate solely on academics."

Derek was glad Gary had to go first, being the pro to Derek's con. This way, at least, Derek's heart had time to calm down. He sat in a chair at the side of Mr. Laithwaite's desk, facing the class, while Gary stood in front of it and addressed the room:

"Mr. Laithwaite, fellow students, I put to you the proposition that schools like ours should not be in the business of fun and games, but of serious study. Math. Science. Languages. Literature. History. These are the things schools are meant to teach. Not how to become Mr. or Miss Universe, or to win some cheap trophy that will gather dust in a closet for a lifetime!"

The whole class cracked up, warming to Gary's performance. Even Derek joined in—although he knew Gary's success was only making his own job more difficult.

"You might argue, 'What about things like music and art, or physical education?' I grant you, there are some benefits to these kinds of activities. But I would also say, those are all things that could be easily done on our own time, and not cut into the hours that are supposed to be dedicated to our academic advancement."

No one was laughing now. Everyone was watching Gary with rapt attention. Derek was getting more antsy with every passing moment. He glanced up at the clock. Two minutes had gone by. Three more to go, and then it would be *his* turn.

Gulp.

Gary went on, glorying in his chance to show Derek up. "But whatever can be said in favor of music, art, et cetera, *nothing* good can be said about school sports. They don't make you smarter. They don't convey any useful information.

"And social skills? Please. Give me a break. Anyone who's ever seen two teams of maniacs chasing each other around, or knocking each other over—fighting over a *ball*, if you can believe it—anyone watching that chaos, even a visitor from Planet Zorgon in the Nerkle Galaxy, would come to the conclusion that sports make idiots out of otherwise reasonable people."

The class was laughing again now. Derek felt miserable. They were laughing *with* Gary, not *at* him. He was spouting nonsense, and they were eating it up like candy.

"It's *worse* than a waste of time," Gary went on. "It's like some kind of evil drug. It takes innocent young people and makes them lose their senses over a *mere game*! And yet sports are promoted as if they're actually *wholesome*!

"These kids—when they aren't playing sports, they're *watching* sports, which is possibly even *worse*. I mean, have you seen the fans in the stands at some of these ball games? Fans with painted faces and bodies, wild costumes—screaming their lungs out, calling for *blood*. And blood is what they get. Think of all the injuries that happen because of sports."

"Thirty seconds," Mr. Laithwaite said, giving Gary the warning to wrap up his argument.

"That is why I propose that schools like ours take the money they spend on sports teams and events, and put it into academics. Let kids play games that make them smarter—like chess or Go. Let them get exercise running errands for their parents, or walking to and from school instead of taking the bus."

Gary quickly glanced at Mr. Laithwaite, who was about to stop him, so Gary said, "I rest my case. Thank you."

The class whooped and applauded. Even Derek had to give a couple of faint claps on Gary's behalf. It really had been quite a performance.

And now it was *Derek's turn*.

He wished there were a lectern around—like the one his dad had used to prop himself up and hide the fact that his legs were shaking. But there was no lectern here. Nothing for poor Derek to hide behind. Nothing to keep him from melting into a puddle of embarrassment. He stood up and cleared his throat as Gary plopped himself down in the chair and shot Derek a self-satisfied look.

Derek's hands, holding his notes, were shaking. He hoped no one would notice. "Sports," he began, "are not a waste of time. They are a vital part of any kid's education. I know it's true for me at least. Throughout my life, sports have been a major way that I've made friends. Some of those friends, I've had for years."

He looked at Vijay, who leaned forward, nodding encouragement. *He knows how nervous I am,* Derek realized.

"Would we have known each other without sports? Maybe. But we'd never have gotten to know each other *as well.* Sports bring out what's inside of us—the best, and also the worst. But they give us a chance to work on our weak spots and make them stronger. And sports also let us set an example for others with our strengths."

So far so good, he thought. He'd used up only one minute, though. After clearing his throat again, he continued:

"Having a healthy body is just as important as having a healthy mind."

"Louder, Mr. Jeter," Mr. Laithwaite interrupted sternly. "If what you have to say is worth hearing, you need to speak up and make sure you're heard. No mumbling, please."

Derek felt his face go red. Had he really been mumbling? He hadn't noticed. . . . He glanced down at his cards again, trying to collect himself after such a stumbling start.

"Sports teach kids a lot of important things they can use later in life. Like teamwork. When you grow up and get a job, or even start a company, you'll definitely need to work with a team at some point. Having played sports gives you a background in how to work with others toward a goal.

"Sports also teach you how to lose and how to win. You learn about 'being a good sport.' But it's about more than that. Sports teach us how to recognize our mistakes and do better next time; how to use a painful loss to motivate us to try even harder.

"Sports teach you how to be a leader, and how to follow a leader. Sometimes you're the best on the team, and sometimes you're one of the weaker members. But everyone gets a chance to contribute, and a championship team is better than any one of its players."

That sounded okay, he thought. *Two minutes left. . . .*

"Sports also teach us how to get along with other kids, from all kinds of backgrounds, kids with all kinds of personalities. Sports even taught me how to get along with *Gary*!"

That got a laugh, and even Mr. Laithwaite cracked the ghost of a smile.

"Also, playing and watching sports is one of the main ways my family and I spend quality time together. It brings us closer, and that is one of the best things in life. Maybe some families don't like sports, but plenty do.

"And that's not all. Sports was one of the first areas in America that got integrated. When Jackie Robinson made it to the Brooklyn Dodgers, it changed the whole country. If it wasn't for him playing sports, kids like me might never have gotten the chance to dream big. For instance, I couldn't have had my dream of playing for the Yankees someday, if not for baseball getting integrated back then.

"And it goes even further. If sports hadn't been integrated first, classrooms and workplaces might never have gotten there. I might not even be standing here right now, if not for Jackie Robinson and others like him."

"Thirty seconds," said Mr. Laithwaite in his usual monotone.

"And finally," Derek said, hurrying a little so he could get one final point in, "sports are open to not just boys but girls, too. Everyone can learn to compete—and competing opens up new horizons for kids. It gives them something to strive for, to improve at, to work toward."

"And . . . time's up!" Mr. Laithwaite announced.

The applause sounded more polite than enthusiastic. Gary rose from the chair, and Derek sat back down, his arms and legs still shaking, his whole body vibrating like a tuning fork.

But he'd gotten through it! Five whole minutes, and he hadn't embarrassed himself too badly. He'd stumbled over some words, and cleared his throat a lot, and of course he'd dropped his notes—but other than that, acceptable.

Still, he knew he had some catching up to do if he wanted to win this debate. That is, if he wasn't completely laid waste to by Gary's rebuttal.

"Mr. Parnell? Your turn," said the teacher.

"Thank you," Gary said, smiling as he took the stage again. "My opponent credits sports for practically every good thing that's ever happened on earth!" Already the class was laughing. "Integration, the women's movement, world peace, success in life . . ."

He shook his head at the sheer ridiculousness of the notion. "May I just point out that lots of people have succeeded in life—including women *and* people of color—without having anything to do with sports?

"As for having big dreams, does my opponent seriously think his so-called dream of playing for the New York Yankees has any remote scintilla of a chance of coming true?"

Gary paused for the laugh he obviously expected. But the class was silent—except for an uncomfortable murmur.

Gary's words hit Derek with the force of a blow. Suddenly he wasn't nervous anymore. He was *furious*!

Gary kept on pushing his point, though. "It's sheer fantasy, that's all. I think we all need to face *reality* if we're going to grow up and be successful. Does anyone seriously believe that success on the athletic field will get you to the top in real life? Remember, there are only a few thousand professional athletes who make any kind of living.

For everyone else, I repeat: sports are basically a waste of time and energy."

"Thank you, Mr. Parnell. Mr. Jeter?"

Derek got up to speak, completely forgetting to be terrified. "My dream is *my dream*," he began. "*No one* can tell me it's just a fantasy. One day, in the future, we can judge who was right—me or Gary. So I'm not going to talk about what might or might not happen to me. I'm going to tell you what's *already* happened—what's *already true*."

He paused, took a deep breath to calm himself, and continued. "My best friend in the whole world is Vijay over there." Derek nodded toward him, and the whole class turned to see Vijay's wide, brilliant smile.

"When we first met, he'd never played sports, and he was afraid to really try them. Now, years later, he's good at baseball, he's pretty fair at basketball, and he's awesome at soccer. He went from being shy to being the star of the talent show last year. That takes courage—and he would have never had that courage without sports.

"My other best friend, Dave Hennum, didn't know anybody when he moved here, and he had a ton of trouble making friends. What drew us together was sports. And even though he now lives in Hong Kong, we'll be friends forever. *That* would have never happened without sports.

"And then there's my newest best friend, Avery Mullins. She was the first girl to ever play on one of my Little League teams. She took a lot of flak from the guys too, but she showed them she could play as well as them—and by the end of the season, *better* than most of them. She went through a trial by fire, and she came out on top. *That* would never have happened without sports.

"There are a million stories like these. My opponent has made you laugh, but his arguments don't hold up. Participating in sports is a major way we grow up, and since school is about preparing us for the future, I know sports are a critical element of that preparation. Thank you."

The class erupted in cheers and applause. Derek stole a glance at Gary, who had a shocked look on his face.

"Thank you, gentlemen," said Mr. Laithwaite. "You may return to your seats. It's time for us to vote."

Derek and Gary sat back down in their own seats, and each of them was patted on the back by the kids at the surrounding desks.

"All right. Who votes 'pro' for ending school sports?" asked Mr. Laithwaite.

Four hands went up. Derek gasped. *Could it be?*

"Who votes for con?"

Eighteen hands went up. It was *a landslide*!

"Well, gentlemen," said Mr. Laithwaite, "we thank you for a lively debate this afternoon. I think you're both deserving of an A for your efforts. Congratulations. Thank you, class. I think you'll all agree that this has been a fascinating exercise. I hope we've all learned from the experience. And I might add that some of you"—he gave Derek a long look—"might want to consider trying out for the debating team next semester."

Derek looked away quickly. He might have won this time, but he was sure in no hurry to do it again anytime soon—let alone join the debating team!

Gary sat there, stunned and motionless, his mouth wide open, flabbergasted at the injustice of it all. After the final bell rang, he strode up to Derek, his mouth twisted in bitter frustration.

"That vote was *rigged*, Jeter, and you know it!" he said, his face right in Derek's. "Those idiots were never going to vote against sports, no matter how much better I did than you! But you and I know who *really* won. It was *obvious*! You can't deny it!"

"I'm not going to argue with you, Gar," Derek said coolly, one corner of his lips curling upward in a smile. "Winning the popular vote is enough for me."

"*Popular?* Gag me with a spoon! Only *mediocrities* care about being popular!" Gary spun on his heels and walked away, still muttering to himself.

Derek felt a swirling mix of emotions, but above all, sheer relief. It was over! He'd survived! Hey, he'd even *won*, and gotten an A, too!

Even if Gary *had* done a better job of arguing, Derek was sure the points he'd made were good ones. Derek had to laugh at the irony of it all. In one fell swoop Gary had just experienced *both* the thrill of victory *and* the agony of defeat—two of the biggest lessons sports can teach!

Chapter Fifteen

THE LONG ROAD BACK

Two weeks, four midterms, two basketball games, and three baseball practices later, Derek was finally back!

Well, not *totally*. He was fully healed, and the doctor had given him a qualified go-ahead to play, while still recommending that he ease back in slowly.

But here at practice, Coach Russell still wouldn't let him run the bases, *or* play shortstop—in other words, nothing where he would really be putting his calf and ankle to the test.

All Derek could do was play first base—where he'd rarely played before—and take his regular turn at batting practice. That at least was a good thing, because Derek soon reminded everyone that he could hit—clobbering line drives all over the field.

But still, he hadn't been able to play *shortstop* for over four weeks. And now that he really could, Coach wasn't giving him the chance!

Coach Russell surprised them all during their water break by delivering a piece of news: "Gang, we're almost at the end of the fall season, and instead of a final practice I've put together one more game for us." That brought a huge cheer from the players, who were excited to put their new skills to the test in game action again.

"We'll be playing the Red Wings, from Hickory Ridge. You might have heard about them. They came in second in the state last year, which means if we beat 'em, we're not too shabby ourselves, right?"

"RIGHT!" they all shouted.

"The game's on the thirtieth—right before Halloween. So let's get ready to haunt Hickory Ridge! What do you say?"

One more deafening cheer, and the players trotted back out to their positions for the second half of practice.

"Derek, you stay here and do some more hitting," the coach said.

"But I'm fine, Coach. I'm fine, *really*! I can play short."

"Not today, kid. We want to ease you back in, like your doctor recommended, and not risk a serious injury. Okay?"

Derek sighed. Next week's Halloween game would be his last chance this season to reclaim his job at shortstop. If he didn't get to play, how could he prove he belonged there? He wouldn't stand a chance—not even the *ghost* of a chance!

Coach Russell must have noticed how downcast Derek was, because he said, "Okay. Go on out to short, just for a few minutes, and let's see how well you're moving."

"Yes, sir!" Derek was practically jumping up and down with excitement.

The coach whistled Harry in from third to come and hit, then shifted Nate to third from short. "Okay, kid," he told Derek. "Get out there—but if you feel *the least little twinge* in that leg . . ."

"I know, Coach," Derek assured him, already on his way. "I will!"

He got to play short for only twenty minutes. But in that time, Derek was able to test his mobility and strength, and his leg came through with flying colors. He felt satisfied that he was all the way back, but he wondered if he'd shown the coach enough to win the position, or at least play short in the final game.

"Hey, Gio! Wait up!"

Gio, already halfway down the stairs, turned and looked behind him. "'Sup, Jeter?"

They gave each other the Friars' handshake and continued down to the locker room together. "You did really well last game, man," Derek told him. "Best effort of the season."

"Thanks," Gio said, sounding surprised that his rival was praising him.

These past few weeks Derek had sat on the bench and cheered Gio on. He'd watched the other teams for weaknesses and shared his observations with Gio, who would listen silently and then go back out and put Derek's tips to good use.

The Friars currently stood at a healthy 6–1 on the season. If they won their next two games, they'd clinch a playoff spot. The best part was, Derek was about to rejoin the team as a full-time player!

"By the way, Gio, I'm back in the rotation today."

"*Really?* You're *playing*?" Gio seemed taken aback, and less than thrilled. He clearly found the news hard to take. He'd been willing to accept Derek's guidance so long as he stayed on the bench. But now that Derek was competing with him for playing time again? Not so much.

"It doesn't matter who starts," Derek said, heading Gio's thoughts off at the pass. "We've both got to make sure we win, right?"

"Yeah . . . sure. . . ." Gio nodded, his jaw tight, then turned and walked toward the locker room. Derek had to hustle to catch up with him.

"Hey, hey!" Coach Nelson greeted the pair as they entered the locker room, where the rest of the team was already suiting up. "We've got a full bench today—first time in a long while! Welcome back, Jeter!" The team gave Derek a hand and some whoops and hollers.

The coach clapped both Gio and Derek on the back.

"Derek, we're going to go with Gio at the start, okay? We'll get you in there later. Be ready."

"Uh . . . sure, Coach." Derek felt disappointed, and a little surprised. Somehow, although he'd told Gio it didn't matter who started, it still stung that Coach hadn't picked him.

It was suddenly clear to Derek that he was going to have to fight to get back his old starting spot. Because it *wasn't* his anymore. *It was Gio's.*

Derek wondered if he would *ever* get his old job back. While he'd been injured, Gio had guided the team to victory after victory. Gio had even shown that he could play team basketball—when he wanted to.

Earlier in the season he'd pretty much ignored Coach's directions. That was why he'd stayed the backup until Derek got hurt. But as the starter Gio had shown he could learn and change.

Derek was expecting more of the same from him today against Saint Paul's. And he was happy about it, because that meant the team would do well.

But from the first jump ball, Gio was back to his ball-hogging ways. He attempted the team's first four shots—forcing them even though he was well covered—and missed every one.

Something must have shifted inside him when he'd found out Derek was playing again. Maybe it was his competitive instincts—the desire to show he was better than Derek—that had made him revert to the old Gio.

Once the Saint Paul's squad realized what was up, they quickly started mobbing Gio. But he still wouldn't dish the ball off. He turned it over twice—and before they knew what was flying, the Friars were down by eleven to the losing-record Crusaders!

Coach called time-out and put Derek in for Gio. As they passed each other, Derek tried to slap him five, but Gio ignored him, confirming that the bad old days were back again. Derek wasn't happy about it, because now he had to help his team climb out of a deep hole. But in the back of his mind, he realized Gio had given him an opening. This was Derek's chance to show how the point position was meant to be played!

On court with him were the Friars' subs, most of whom hadn't played that much over the course of the season. Derek decided to see what they could do when they got an open shot. He fired a no-look pass to Jake Maroni, the Friars' third-string shooting guard, and the shortest kid on the team. Jake fired, and hit the open jumper!

Nothin' but net, Derek thought, hustling back on defense. His ankle felt normal—a huge relief! Finally he could go full-out and play the game the *right* way!

Derek harassed his man constantly, poking at the ball until he forced a turnover. After dribbling down the court, he lobbed one up to Charlie Wong for an easy layup!

Saint Paul's tried a set play next, but Derek was one step ahead of them. Anticipating a cross-court pass, he intercepted it. This time he was ahead of the pack and laid it up himself for his first points in weeks!

The Crusaders' coach called time-out. Their lead was already down to five, and Derek had only been in there for two minutes!

"Way to go, Jeter," said Coach Nelson, patting him on the back. "Your leg feeling okay?"

"It's fine," Derek said quickly, hoping Coach wasn't going to sit him down already.

"Great. Great. Keep it up, kid. Let's get the lead back."

Derek went back out onto the court, this time with Sam, Marcus, and the rest of the usual starters. He was now able to feed the ball to the team's best scorers. By halftime the Friars were in the lead. And even though it was only a one-point advantage, Derek felt like he'd gotten the job done.

He thought for sure he'd made a good impression with his unselfish play and stellar results—even though he'd only scored two points himself—so he was surprised when Coach Nelson sent Gio out to start the second half.

"Hey," Derek called out to him as he was about to get back onto the court.

Gio turned. "Yeah?"

"Good luck, man. Go get 'em."

Gio nodded, unsmiling. "Yeah. Thanks."

"And hey—try to get Marcus some looks too, huh?"

Derek knew Gio might react badly to any advice from

him, even though he'd been happy to take it while Derek was injured. But since Marcus was Gio's best friend, Derek figured Gio might give the idea some consideration.

With Gio back in, Saint Paul's went right back to double-teaming him. They'd played straight man-to-man against Derek because he hadn't been trying to do it all by himself.

But this time when the double-team came, Gio bounced a no-look pass right to Marcus under the basket. *Two points!* The whole Friars bench rose to their feet and cheered.

And that was just the beginning. Gio seemed to have flipped a switch. Now the Crusaders didn't know where the ball was going next. The Friars kept getting open looks and scoring easy buckets. They were even looking livelier on defense!

Soon St. Augustine had a double-digit lead. By now the Crusaders had stopped double-teaming Gio. Covered one-on-one, he was able to isolate, drive the lane for his own buckets, or dish off if help came. He wound up scoring ten points in the second half alone, and leading the Friars to an easy but important win.

Derek played only two minutes in the second half, to give Gio a brief rest. Afterward Coach Nelson told him he hadn't wanted to push Derek too hard his first game back, especially since the game had been well in hand toward the end.

Derek understood, even though he was disappointed. It had probably been wise to ease him back into game action. Besides, even playing limited minutes, he'd had an impact, reversing the momentum in the first half. And also by what he'd said to Gio. Derek was convinced that his words had influenced Gio's change of approach in the second half.

Sure enough, just then Gio walked past and said, "Nice advice."

"You're welcome," Derek replied, smiling. "One more game and we're in the playoffs, man. Let's keep it going, no matter who's out there."

A brief dark cloud seemed to pass over Gio's face—and then it left. He offered Derek his hand and said, "Same team."

"Same team," Derek repeated.

Chapter Sixteen

BACK IN THE GAME

Derek could feel the excitement buzzing through his body as he got out of the car and ran toward home plate. *Finally!* A real baseball game—his first in months!

All season long he'd dreamed of this day. But when Coach Russell spoke to the team before the contest, Derek's fantasies were brought abruptly back down to earth.

"I know some of you are wondering why I've been switching up positions the last few weeks. I just want to say, no matter where you wind up playing come spring, you're all vital to this team we're building. Every position is equally important—and that includes alternate."

No one said anything, but furtive looks were exchanged all along the bench.

"For today, against the Red Wings, we're going to switch things around every two innings, so you'll have a chance to show your stuff at more than one position. Where you play during this game isn't necessarily where you'll play going forward. And I won't be making any final decisions today either. Lots of things can change between now and April. But you're all going to be on this team come spring season, no matter what. Clear?"

Everyone nodded.

"Good. That's all for now. Let's go get 'em."

Derek braced himself for the challenge. He knew he was "on the bubble," as the saying went. Today's game was going to be about impressing the coaches, particularly at shortstop. But would two innings be enough for him to prove himself?

Oh, well. At least he was healthy again. That was all he could ask for, except maybe a few spectacular plays at short and a few big hits.

As far as the other kids went, Derek couldn't really wish them bad luck. Everyone on this team had become friends over the past two months. But Derek didn't want to be outshone, either, so it was up to him to concentrate, focus, and give it his absolute best.

He searched the stands and spotted his family. There was Sharlee, seated in between his mom and dad. But whom was his mom talking to?

Suddenly Derek realized that his entire fan club was

there—including Vijay, Avery, and her mom, who must have driven them there. And they'd all come to root for *him*!

Derek felt hugely grateful. He swore to himself he wouldn't let them down. But to his frustration, he wound up starting the game on the bench, while Nate played short, Mo started at third, and Eli manned second base.

Derek sure hoped that didn't reflect where they stood with the coach, but he had to believe it did. As he'd been taking time to heal, he'd had to watch while the other three had lots of chances to impress the coach, which they'd obviously done.

Derek found it difficult to sit still as the game began, especially since the West Siders quickly fell behind to the Red Wings, 2–0, on a walk and a pair of solid doubles to left. Even though Harry got out of the jam without further trouble, it was not a good way to start.

On top of that the first half of the inning ended on a nifty play by Nate at short. He caught a line drive, then threw to second to double up the runner before he could get back to the base.

Luckily, the West Siders quickly got both runs back, on a single, a walk, and a double by Nate, who was clearly the team's best power hitter. Derek found himself almost jumping out of his skin to get into the game.

The second inning featured Mo starting a sparkling double play at third, and Harry retiring the side without trouble. But the opposing pitcher held the bottom of the West Siders' order without a hit, so the second inning ended with the game tied, 2–2.

"Okay, Jeter, you're in at short," said Coach Russell. Nate shifted over to his old position at third, Mo moved to second, and Eli sat down, still hopeful of winning a regular position on the team.

"Hit it to me. . . . Hit it to me," Derek kept repeating under his breath.

He needed some chances in the field, to show what he could do! And when Harry struck out the first two batters, Derek was afraid his two innings would go by without any action coming his way at all!

Harry walked the next batter on a full count. Watching and waiting, Derek realized that no matter how much he loved basketball, baseball would always be his first and most important sport. He was more sure of it now than ever before, and being on the West Siders all next spring and summer had him incredibly psyched. But he didn't want to go in as the alternate—or even at second or third.

Is Harry ever going to let them put the bat on the ball? he wondered.

SMACK!

A hard line drive sizzled toward Derek's head and to his left. Derek took three running steps, leapt, and made the grab!

"WHOA!" everyone shouted, and the West Siders and

their fans gave it up for Derek big-time as he jogged back to the bench.

Coach Russell clapped him on the back. "Attaboy!"

Derek felt a thrill go through him, but there was no time to reflect on what he'd just done. He was on deck!

Harry slashed a single the other way on the first pitch he saw, past the diving second baseman. Before Derek could even get ready mentally, he was standing in the batter's box.

He glanced down the line at the third-base coach—and was stunned to see him give the bunt signal!

In travel baseball bunting and stealing were allowed. Derek and his teammates had been working on both for weeks, and now he was being asked to bunt Harry over.

Derek was disappointed to see the sign. If he was successful, he'd have used up one of his precious at bats just to bunt. But he also knew that Harry wasn't a fast runner, and in a tie game every run was precious. That was why Harry wasn't being asked to steal.

Derek let the first pitch go by for a ball, pulling the bat back from bunting position. The fielders, having seen Derek square around, moved in closer for the second pitch, expecting the bunt now.

Derek was disappointed to get the bunt sign again. But this time he got a pitch he could handle, and laid one down along the third-base line. He took off like a shot, expecting a close play, but he reached without a throw, then looked around to see what had happened.

The third baseman had been waiting for the ball to roll foul, and finally got his reward. Just before the ball stopped rolling, it veered to the left and went foul.

Noooo! Derek thought, rolling his eyes.

Back to the drawing board. On the other hand, now he had another chance to get a hit! At least he hoped so. . . .

But no. The third-base coach flashed the bunt sign again. Derek took ball two, then ball three. With the count at 3–1, he finally got the green light to swing away.

Derek told himself to stay calm and not get too excited. He reminded himself to take a deep breath and focus on the pitcher's release point.

Here it came—a fastball right down the middle. Derek was expecting it, since the last thing the pitcher wanted was to walk him. He swung, and laced a savage line drive that landed between the left and center fielders and rolled all the way to the fence!

Harry came around to score the go-ahead run for the West Siders. Derek was about to slide into third when Coach Richie gave him the sign to keep going!

Derek kicked it into a higher gear as he rounded the base. He could hear yelling and screaming, and knew the throw would be coming—but he also knew it would have to be perfect to get him.

He saw the catcher lean to his left to receive the relay. Derek slid wide to the right, avoiding the tag by inches to score the team's fourth run—on an inside-the-park homer!

The Red Wings got out of the inning without any further damage, and Derek went out to play short for his second and last turn there. This time the action came right at him, in the form of a broken-bat fly ball to short left.

Derek started backpedaling, then turned and ran, looking over his shoulder. Finally he reached out, grabbed the ball in the webbing of his glove, and tumbled head over heels, barely hanging on to it!

As the sound of cheers filled the air, Derek could feel himself swell with pride and satisfaction. But he still had a game to play, and nobody had guaranteed him the shortstop position yet.

Harry began to falter. He gave up a homer, a double, and a game-tying single before recovering his location and retiring the last two hitters on strikeouts.

Derek headed back to the bench. His chance at shortstop was over, but he hoped the coaches wouldn't soon forget it.

The game remained tied at 4–4. Derek put in his time at third base without seeing any action come his way. His next time up, in the fifth, he hit a clean double down the right field line, though the inning ended with him stranded at second.

When the score remained tied after the regulation six innings, the two teams' coaches conferred, then announced that they'd agreed to play up to three extra innings to decide the game!

This was great news as far as Derek was concerned, and it turned even greater when Coach told him that because it was extra innings, instead of rotating to second he'd be back at short for the rest of the day!

The seventh inning saw both teams going down one, two, three. In the top of the eighth the Red Wings put two men on with nobody out. Mo was pitching now—not his best spot, but Harry had reached his pitch limit and was now at third base.

The next hitter moved both runners over with a sacrifice bunt. Mo walked the bases loaded, and the Red Wings' cleanup man came up to bat.

He fouled off the first pitch, just missing on a mighty swing. Derek backed up to the inner edge of the outfield grass, preparing for the double play to end the Red Wings' half of the inning. It paid off when, on the next pitch, the hitter smacked a sharp grounder that had Mo skipping to get out of the way.

Derek got a great jump, dived, and came up with the ball. Without taking it out of his mitt, he flipped to Nate at second for one out. Nate turned and fired to first to complete the double play—and the top of the inning was over!

Now it was Derek's turn to lead off. The first pitch nearly hit him, and he had to spin out of the way. After a called strike he managed to work the count to 3–1.

Here he was again, one more time, in a hitter's count. The pitch was high, up in his eyes, and Derek nearly came out of his shoes trying to hit another homer and win the game for his team.

But he whiffed, and now the count was full.

Derek knew that his job as the leadoff man was to reach base no matter what. All thoughts of the long ball vanished from his head, and he concentrated just on making solid contact.

The fielders were playing him to pull. That encouraged Derek to wait on the pitch and go the other way. Swinging, he led with his hands the way Coach Russell had taught them, letting the bat trail behind for an inside-out swing.

The result was a soft line drive between the first and second basemen. It trickled into the outfield for a single!

Nate came up to bat next. Derek looked over to third base and saw the coach give the steal sign! Derek took off like a flash on the next pitch, and slid into second just a hair ahead of the tag.

"Safe!" cried the umpire.

Derek could smell the win now. A measly single to the outfield would bring him home with the winning run!

With the count at 1–2 the pitcher fired one low in the dirt, and it got by the catcher. Derek made it to third without a throw! *Still* nobody out, and Derek only a base away from victory.

But on the next pitch Nate struck out. So did the next hitter. If Mo couldn't get a hit, the game would keep going for another inning, and the victory would still be up for grabs.

But Mo was up to the task. With the count at 2–1 he sent a fly ball into short center that dropped just in front of the onrushing outfielders.

Because there were two outs, Derek had been running on contact. He sprinted home, and when the ball landed, he was already standing on home plate, cheering along with everyone else on the West Siders' side of the field.

Game over! They'd done it!

Even as he celebrated with his teammates, Derek knew that the shortstop position was still undecided, and that none of them would know till spring where they'd be playing.

Nate and Eli had both played well at short, but Derek knew that at least he'd been at his very best and shown off every part of his game.

Vijay greeted him with a high five, and Avery gave him a hug. "That was awesome!" she told him. "*You* were awesome!"

"Fantastic!" Vijay agreed. "You are seriously ready for the big leagues!"

Derek had to laugh. "Cut it out, Vij. You're embarrassing me. Quit exaggerating."

Vijay laughed. "Well, you certainly are on your way."

That much, Derek could allow. One thing he was sure of—today had been a very good day in his baseball life. And a very *important* one too.

Chapter Seventeen

THE BRASS RING

The Friars were on the bus, headed for Northeast Junior High, when Coach Nelson called for quiet. Gio and Marcus, goofing around in the back seats, had to be asked twice.

"Today's the biggest game we've played so far, guys—and it's got to be our best. If we win, we're in—a guaranteed playoff spot. If we lose . . . Well, we're not going to lose. Right?"

"RIGHT!" all the kids yelled.

"Just to paint the picture for you," the coach went on, "we've got three games after this—against the best three teams in the league that aren't called the Friars—so let's win tonight and seal the deal. Right?"

"RIGHT!" the answer came again.

"Okay, so today's starting lineup: we've got Marcus at center, Jose and Tyquan at forward, Sam . . ."

Derek held his breath. Would Coach name him, or Gio?

". . . and Derek at point."

Everyone started talking at once. Derek turned to see the shock on Gio's face, and he knew what must have been going on in his head.

As soon as they got off the bus, on the way into the visitors' locker room, Derek caught up with him. "Hey, can I talk to you for a second?"

Gio gave him a dull, hostile look. "What for? You got what you wanted, didn't you?".

"That's what I want to talk to you about," Derek said, holding Gio's gaze.

Gio glanced at Marcus, who was standing silently by, looking embarrassed.

And why not? thought Derek. Here was Marcus, in the middle of a conflict he wanted nothing to do with between his best friend and his starting point guard.

Gio motioned to Derek, and they went off to the side, far enough to be out of earshot.

"Listen, I know how you must be feeling," Derek began.

"No, you don't. You *think* you do. I'm totally cool with it, so there's nothing to talk about."

Derek could tell Gio was lying. But he needed to break through Gio's armor, for the good of the team. He needed Gio to play *team ball*.

"You know, Gio, I was in your exact position last year, in AAU ball. I had to deal with being a sub, even though I thought I was better than the starter. But that kid was the team captain, so I took my cues from him. I saw him dishing off, even when he had a shot. I saw him hustling for every rebound, looking to get everyone involved in the offense. So when I did get to play—which wasn't often—I tried to do the same."

"So . . . you're saying *what* exactly?"

"I know you're the most talented player on the team—more talented than I am—and so does Coach. But *he's* making the decisions. He's our *leader*. We're never going to win a championship if we're not all pulling together."

"You're not the coach," Gio said bitterly.

"No, of course not! But you know he would say the same thing. He's *already* said it, more than once."

"You finished?"

"Yeah. I'm done."

"Good. Me too. Now let's go get changed."

Derek followed him into the locker room, hoping against hope that his words had made a dent.

As they strode into the gym, Derek looked up at the bleachers, trying to find his parents and sister. He spotted them—and there were Avery and Vijay again, with Sharlee sitting happily between them!

"DE-REK!" she yelled, her voice piercing the hubbub.

Derek smiled and waved back. He was really touched that his friends had made it all the way to Northeast Junior High, which was far from the west side, where the Jeters and Vijay lived.

Derek didn't see Avery's mom. Vijay's parents weren't there either, so it must have been his own mom and dad who'd driven them here—and kept it a secret to surprise him! Well, that got his mind off his problems with Gio, all right. Derek was determined to show his favorite people what he could do on the court!

His main job was to get things rolling for the Friars. But the Lions of Northeast Junior High started off on a shooting hot streak. Even with Friars defenders in their faces, they sank three quick shots, while St. Augustine had just two points, on a pair of free throws by Sam.

Derek knew the Lions wouldn't stay that hot all game— no team ever did. All the Friars had to do was keep getting in their faces, making them rush their shots or take off-balance jumpers. The tide would turn eventually, he was sure of it.

He saw that whomever he passed to was instantly double-teamed. The Lions had already forced three turnovers, though Derek himself hadn't committed one.

So instead of dishing off, or passing it off on the pick-and-roll, Derek drove all the way to the basket himself for a surprisingly easy layup!

There! Make the Lions cover him, or else take the shot.

It's not selfish if I'm the open man, he told himself. *Never mind what Gio thinks. If Coach doesn't approve, he'll tell me himself, or sit me down.*

Midway through the first half, Derek had racked up twelve points on his own. He was the high scorer for the Friars, who'd turned the tables on the Lions and now led by six.

Coach Nelson sent Gio into the game, giving Derek a well-deserved rest. "How's that leg doing?" Coach asked him, yelling over the crowd noise.

Derek gave him a big smile and two thumbs-up.

"That's my guy!" Coach said. "Way to play smart!" Turning away, he cupped his hands to his mouth and yelled, "Go get 'em, Gio!"

"Go, Gio!" Derek echoed.

Gio could handle the ball better than anyone else his age that Derek had ever seen. The talent was unmistakable. But he usually gummed it up with his stubborn, selfish attitude. Now, though—whether it was Derek calling him out, or something else—Gio began to play the unselfish style he'd exhibited sporadically while Derek had been sidelined.

He found Marcus with a dazzling lob pass for a layup. Then he snuck up behind the Lions' point guard and knocked the ball loose for a turnover. Sam converted the steal into two points—nothing but net—and suddenly the Friars had a double-digit lead!

By halftime the lead had ballooned to thirteen, at 41–28. And in the second half the story was much the same. Gio started out on the bench, but when he came in, he ran the offense the way Coach Nelson had taught them in practice.

When Coach finally put the third-string point guard in for the final two minutes, Gio and Derek high-fived each other in front of the bench, all smiles now.

"We okay?" Derek asked, just to make sure.

Gio nodded. "We're good, man. Point taken."

Derek breathed a sigh of relief and turned to watch the final seconds tick off the clock. The Northeast crowd was quiet as the buzzer sounded, but Derek's fan club was whooping it up like there was no tomorrow!

The Friars all embraced in a big circle. "My guys!" Coach Nelson exulted. "We're in! And if we keep playing like we did today, we're going win this division, and rip right through the district playoffs too!"

Everyone cheered, then headed back to the locker room—except Derek, who went over to greet his cheering section. "I can't believe you guys are here!" he told Vijay and Avery.

"Your folks drove us," Avery explained.

"Great game, Derek!" Vijay said excitedly.

"Vij," Derek said, putting an arm around Vijay's shoulders. "Hey, man. Now that baseball season's over, we can start spending more time together, huh?"

"It feels like years," Vijay said.

"Hey, you two, cut it short," Mrs. Jeter said. "Derek, go get changed and come back out. We're all going to Dairy Queen for sundaes to celebrate!"

"All of us?" Derek said.

"Good thing we still have the old station wagon," Mr. Jeter said with a wide grin. "It seats six people, comfortably."

"Ugh . . . I can't eat another bite. . . ." Derek stared at the mound of half-melted ice cream still staring him in the face. He pushed it away. "I'm done. Defeated by the extra-large banana split."

"I knew you couldn't finish it," Sharlee said, pulling it toward her.

"Oh, no you don't," Mrs. Jeter said, steering it back away from Sharlee. "You've already had enough for one sitting—or *three*."

"Awww." Sharlee's disappointment was more show than real.

"Derek," said his dad, "I want you to know how proud Mom and I are of you. You really managed to take on a lot these past two months, and mostly you handled it all well."

"Except for letting myself get hurt and missing half of it," Derek said, shaking his head.

"Hey, injuries happen," Avery said.

"Nah. I should've taken better care when it first happened. You know, let it heal."

"From here on in," Mrs. Jeter said, "you'll need to make sure you have some time to relax—and when you're hurt, time for your body to recover."

"Just like Kurt Carsten," Mr. Jeter said. "Now I've got to watch the Red Sox in the playoffs, while my guys go home for the winter. Anyway, Derek, I hope you learned something from the experience."

"I did, Dad. I learned you can still be a leader, even when you're not playing. But I have to say I never want to do it again!"

Everyone laughed, but Derek had more to say. "I mean, I'm glad I signed up for both sports at once, because I learned *so much*—like how to be a leader sometimes, and how to follow the leader other times. But I've got to admit, it was kind of an ordeal—especially doing the debate in the middle of it all."

"So, what happens next year?" Vijay asked nervously. "Are you going to play both sports again?"

"Well, baseball's my heart and soul. If I have to choose, it's always going to come first. But I don't see why I shouldn't do both."

"I knew you'd say that," Vijay said, smiling.

"I've just got to make sure I pay attention to my body, and listen when it's trying to tell me something."

"Well, it's getting late," said Mrs. Jeter, waving for the

waiter to bring the check. "We'd better get your friends home."

"Hey," Avery said, "do you guys want to get together this weekend?"

"Sure!" Derek said. "It's been too long for sure!"

"It's supposed to rain both days," Vijay said.

"Well, then . . . how about we go bowling or something?" Avery suggested.

"Great idea!" Derek and Vijay said together.

"Mom? Dad?" Derek asked.

"I'm sure we can make it happen," said Mrs. Jeter. "Don't you think so, Charles?"

"Mmm . . . I don't see why not. So long as Sharlee can come too."

"YAY!" Sharlee said, clapping her hands.

Derek, Vijay, and Avery all exchanged high fives.

"Yes!" Derek said. "We've got a plan!" He sat there, basking in the glow of family and friendship.

Winter was on the way, and baseball was done until spring. But there was always a sport to play, as long as you had good friends to play it with!

JETER'S LEADERS

is a leadership development program created to empower, recognize, and enhance the skills of high school students who:

- **PROMOTE HEALTHY LIFESTYLES AND ARE FREE OF ALCOHOL AND SUBSTANCE ABUSE**

- **ACHIEVE ACADEMICALLY**

- **ARE COMMITTED TO IMPROVING THEIR COMMUNITY THROUGH SOCIAL CHANGE ACTIVITIES**

- **SERVE AS ROLE MODELS TO YOUNGER STUDENTS AND DELIVER POSITIVE MESSAGES TO THEIR PEERS**

"Your role models should teach you, inspire you, criticize you, and give you structure. My parents did all of these things with their contracts. They tackled every subject. There was nothing we didn't discuss. I didn't love every aspect of it, but I was mature enough to understand that almost everything they talked about made sense." —DEREK JETER

DO YOU HAVE WHAT IT TAKES TO BECOME A
JETER'S LEADER?

- I am drug and alcohol free.
- I volunteer in my community.
- I am good to the environment.
- I am a role model for kids.
- I do not use the word "can't."
- I am a role model for my peers and younger kids.
- I stand up for what's right.

- I am respectful to others.
- I encourage others to participate.
- I am open-minded.
- I set my goals high.
- I do well in school.
- I like to exercise and eat well to keep my body strong.
- I am educated on current events.

CREATE A CONTRACT

What are your goals?

Sit down with your parents or an adult mentor to create your own contract to help you take the first step toward achieving your dreams.

For more information on JETER'S LEADERS, visit
TURN2FOUNDATION.ORG

About the Authors

DEREK JETER played Major League Baseball for the New York Yankees for twenty seasons, during which time he won five World Series. Considered one of the greatest shortstops of all time, Derek has been a role model to young people on the field and off—thanks largely to the work of his Turn 2 Foundation. (For more information, visit mlb.com/turn-2-foundation.) Though he grew up in Kalamazoo, Michigan, he often envisioned himself playing shortstop for the Yankees. Derek knows the power of a dream.

PAUL MANTELL is the author of more than one hundred books for young readers.

BULLYING.
BE A LEADER AND STOP IT.

Do your part to stop bullies in their tracks.

Protect yourself and your friends with STOPit. It's easy.
It's anonymous. It's the right thing to do.

"Never let a bully win." - Derek Jeter

Download the app today!

TURN 2 FOUNDATION, INC.

STOP!T

TURN THE PAGE FOR A SNEAK PEEK AT

WALK-OFF.

NEW YORK TIMES BESTSELLING AUTHOR

DEREK JETER

WALK-OFF

"That ball was outside!" Derek Jeter sprang up from his seat on the living room couch, his arms outstretched in protest. "Dad, that ump needs glasses."

"Now, Derek, that was a borderline pitch," Mr. Jeter replied, gazing at the TV screen as the dejected Tigers batter headed back to the dugout. "Give the umps a little slack. It's a hard job."

"I think the hitter should have swung," said Derek's little sister, Sharlee. Over the winter she'd become obsessed with baseball, and hitting in particular, mostly because their dad had started taking her along when he and Derek went to the indoor batting cages to practice.

"Who was that batter, anyway? I never saw him before," Derek said.

"Jim Faye," said Mr. Jeter. "He was in the minors last year."

"There are so many new guys on the team," Derek complained, sinking back down into his seat. "I barely know who's who now. Where are all the guys from last year?"

"Well, they traded some away, let others go to free agency. The Tigers are rebuilding, Derek."

"Why? They had a great team a couple of seasons ago."

"Well, things change, Son. It's a new season. New players, and a nice clean slate, too. Everyone's in first place on opening day. Speaking of which, are you two excited for your leagues to start up next weekend?"

"Yes!" Sharlee exulted, bouncing up and down in her chair. "I can't wait. I'm going to hit a home run every game this year!"

"She does have a mean swing," Mr. Jeter said, glancing at Derek with a wink.

Derek laughed. "Hey, I'm just glad to get on the field again after all this time. It feels like years."

Derek really was feeling jazzed about the new season. First and foremost he was now on the travel team. And unlike last fall, when practically all they'd done was practice, this spring would bring a whole slew of games against the stiffest competition in the region.

It made Derek feel like he was an elite player—at least in Kalamazoo. Of course, his dreams were much bigger.

He wanted to be the best, not just in Kalamazoo but in the whole country.

On top of travel baseball, Derek would also be playing his final season in Junior League. Next year, in eighth grade, he'd move up to the Senior League, where the players were older, bigger, taller, faster, and stronger.

Derek himself had grown four inches over the past winter. If he kept it up, he might even get to be six feet tall, which would be really cool. Onward and upward, that was how he looked at it. Every day brought a new challenge, and he would work as hard as necessary to be ready.

"Derek!" his mom called from the kitchen. "Sharlee! Anyone going to clean up in here?"

Derek and Sharlee hopped up and went to help. Their chores around the house were all laid out in the contracts they'd signed with their parents. In exchange for privileges, they had clear responsibilities, and doing dishes after meals was one of them.

"There are so many leftovers," Sharlee complained as she and Derek packed them up for later.

"Easter Sunday lunch," their mom remarked, shrugging. "Should I have just made peanut butter sandwiches?"

"No!" Derek and Sharlee said at once, and they all laughed. Their mom had made a heaping feast, and Derek couldn't imagine eating again till at least Tuesday.

"You guys ready to go back to school tomorrow?" Mrs. Jeter asked.

"Yes!" said Derek.

"No," said Sharlee at the same time.

"What's wrong?" Derek asked his sister. "You just had ten days off, didn't you?"

"But it's springtime," Sharlee explained. "Finally. I want to be outside. Why can't we have classes out on the lawn?"

"When you're in charge of the schools, you can make those decisions," Mrs. Jeter said, patting Sharlee on the shoulder. "And don't forget to dry the frying pan."

Sharlee moaned, but did as she was told.

Derek had had the same ten days off, but Sharlee had been hanging out with her friends the whole time. Ciara had been at their house almost every day over the break, and so had the Parker triplets—London, Adriana, and Abby. They'd driven Derek crazy with their talking and laughing and playing all kinds of games he wasn't interested in.

His own best friend, Vijay, had been away with his parents, visiting family in India the whole time. Derek's other best friend, Dave, had moved to Hong Kong with his parents the year before. His friend Avery, who lived across town, had gone traveling with her mom over Easter week, so Derek had spent a lot of time alone, getting a head start on reading assignments for school.

Last term he'd fallen behind in his schoolwork while playing both basketball and baseball. He'd done fine on his final grades, but not without a lot of hard work cramming at the last minute. He was determined to get ahead of the game this time around, because playing in two baseball leagues at once was going to eat up a lot of time between now and the end of June.

"Can I go over to the Hill?" Derek asked his mom. "I think Vijay might be home by now."

"Sure," said his mom. "Give him my best. Be back by six, okay?"

"We're actually eating *supper* tonight? After *that lunch? Seriously?*"

"You're a growing boy, old man," his mom said with a wry smile. "You're full now, but you've been basically a bottomless pit the last six months."

He could tell she was happy that he'd gotten taller. For the longest time it had seemed like every other kid but him was growing into a man. Now he'd joined the party.

On the other hand, in a couple of months he'd be an actual teenager. The thought of it made him uncomfortable, and a little sad. Why did things always have to change? Why couldn't life stay like it had been his whole life?

Vijay was already out on Jeter's Hill (named for Derek because he spent almost every free minute there, playing ball). Vijay was playing catch with Harry Hicks, who also lived at Mount Royal Townhouses and whom Derek had known since he was a little kid.

Derek had never been happier to see his best buddy. They exchanged hugs and high fives with their mitts, and their elaborate secret handshake with their throwing hands.

Harry came over to greet him. "Hey, Jeter," he said.

"How was Disneyland?" Derek asked him. Harry and his family had just returned from the West Coast, he knew.

"Awesome, but I might have outgrown some of the stuff," Harry admitted. "My little sister went crazy for it, though."

"So would mine," Derek said, thinking of Sharlee and remembering how excited she'd gotten at that water park in New Jersey last summer.

"Hey, are you on the Yankees this season?" Harry asked him.

"No," said Derek. "The Reds."

"Bummer," said Harry. "Hey, I've got to go. My grandma's coming over this afternoon. See you guys in school." Harry took off at a trot, checking his wristwatch.

"How about you, Vij? What team are you on?"

"Oh . . . me?" Vijay had a funny look on his face, almost like he was suddenly shy.

"You see anyone else here?"

"Um, I'm not playing ball this year," Vijay said softly, looking away.

"Say *what*?" Derek couldn't believe his ears. "But . . . we've been on the same team every year since . . ."

"Since the beginning," Vijay said, nodding. "But for every beginning there's an end."

"You mean you're not going to play ball again? Ever?"

"Well, like, here on the Hill, of course I'll still play. But I'm just . . . I don't know. . . ."

Derek wanted to press the issue—to ask Vijay why. He just couldn't understand.

Vijay had improved greatly over his years in Little League. He'd started as a complete novice and had wound up being an asset to the team. But he'd never been one of the better players. And while many of the kids had started their growth spurts already, Vijay hadn't grown much at all the past year or so. He still looked for all the world like a fifth grader.

"Remember that kid last spring, who got his arm broken by a fastball?" Vijay reminded Derek.

Derek nodded. "He wasn't on our team, but we all signed his cast anyway."

"I'll bet he's not playing ball anymore either. I wouldn't want to get hit like that. Some of the pitchers are six feet tall!"

It suddenly hit Derek that Vijay was really quitting the game. "Gee," he said, feeling suddenly emotional. "It won't be the same without you."

"You'll do fine," Vijay assured him. "You've got what it takes, Derek. You always have, and you keep getting better every year. I've kind of hit my ceiling, if you know what I mean."

Derek wanted to argue with him further, but Vijay preempted him. "Anyway, don't feel bad on my account. I've got a new passion."

"Oh yeah? What?"

"Are you ready?" Vijay asked, as if he were about to reveal the secret of the universe. Spreading his hands out and smiling blissfully, he said, "Video games!"

"Video games?" Derek repeated, confused.

"Derek, it's a whole new world. No, a whole new *universe*. Wait till you try them."

"I've tried them," Derek said. "A couple of times. I think it was over at Jeff Jacobson's house. *Super Something Brothers*. . . . It was pretty fun."

"Super MARIO Brothers," Vijay corrected him. "And now I have my own game console at home."

"Wow, really?"

"My parents got it for me for my birthday, right before we left for India. I took it with me, and I was playing it half the time there. My parents even yelled at me because I was ignoring my cousins to play it. But, Derek, you can't believe how much fun it is!"

"Well, next time I'm over at your house . . ."

"Totally. And guess what? Now there's actually a real video game store in town, where you can go and play all these games on gigantic screens, and you can win tickets to redeem for prizes, and you can blow your entire allowance in one afternoon of supreme ecstasy!"

Derek had to laugh. He knew Vijay was joking, but he also knew that his friend meant every word. Vijay had already probably blown an insane amount of chore money at the new arcade.

Derek had seen the place from the outside—it was right across the street from the batting cages—but he'd never been inside. He couldn't imagine having time for video games.

After playing catch with Vijay, Derek walked home feeling dejected. He'd been so excited about playing in two leagues, one with old friends and the other with new ones. But without his best pal, Little League baseball wouldn't be what he had envisioned.

Last fall he'd worn himself out playing basketball and baseball at the same time. In fact, he'd wound up getting hurt and missing substantial chunks of the season.

Maybe I should just do travel team, he thought. Multiple games a week for the next two months was a lot, for sure. And travel back and forth ate up a lot of time too.

On the other hand, the more baseball he played, the better he would get—right? Derek was confident he could handle it, and also get his schoolwork done.

But it just wouldn't be the same without Vijay.

Read all the books in the Derek Jeter Contract series:

THE CONTRACT

HIT & MISS

CHANGE UP

FAIR BALL

CURVEBALL

FAST BREAK

STRIKE ZONE

WIND UP

SWITCH-HITTER

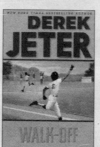

WALK-OFF